THE GARLAND LIBRARY OF SCIENCE FICTION

A collection of 45 works
of science fiction
selected by Lester del Rey,
with a separate introductory volume,
Science Fiction, 1926-1976,
written by him,
especially for this series.

Garland Publishing, Inc., New York & London
1975

Library of Congress Cataloging in Publication Data

Farmer, Philip José.
   Night of light.

   (The Garland library of science fiction)
   Reprint of the ed. published by Berkley Pub. Corp.,
New York.
   I. Title. II. Series.
[PZ4.F234Ni5]   [PS3556.A72]   813'.5'4   75-404
ISBN 0-8240-1409-X

NIGHT OF LIGHT

Philip José Farmer

A BERKLEY MEDALLION BOOK
Published by
BERKLEY PUBLISHING CORPORATION

PART ONE

On earth it would be a fearful thing to see a man chasing down the street after the skin from a human face, a thin layer of tissue blown about like a piece of paper by the wind.

On the planet of Dante's Joy the sight aroused only a mild wonder in the few passersby. And they were interested because the chaser was an Earthman and, therefore, a curiosity in himself.

John Carmody ran down the long straight street, past the clifflike fronts of towers built of huge blocks of quartz-shot granite, with gargoyles and nightmare shapes grinning from the darkened interiors of many niches and with benedictions of god and goddess leaning from the many balconies.

A little man, dwarfed even more by the soaring walls and flying buttresses, he ran down the street in frantic pursuit of the fluttering transparent skin that turned over and over as it sailed upon the strong wind, over and over, showing the eye holes, the earholes, the sagging empty gaping mouthhole, and trailing a few long and blond hairs from the line of the forehead, the scalp itself being absent.

The wind howled behind him, seeming to add its fury to his. Suddenly the skin, which had fluttered just within his reach, shot upwards on a strong draft coming around a building.

Carmody cursed and leaped, and his fingers touched the thing. But it flew up and landed on a balcony at least ten feet above him, lodged against the feet of the diorite image of the god Yess.

Panting, holding his aching sides, John Carmody leaned against the base of a buttress. Though he had once been in superb condition, as befitted the ex-welterweight amateur boxing champion of the Federation, his belly was swelling to make room for his increasing appetite, and fat was building up beneath his chin, like a noose.

It made little difference to him or to anybody else. He was not much to look at, anyway. He had a shock of blue-black hair, stiff and straight, irresistibly reminding one of a porcupine's quills. His head was melon-shaped, his forehead

5

too high, his left eyelid drooped just enough to give his face a lopsided look, his nose was too long and sharp, his mouth too thin, his teeth too widely spaced.

He looked up at the balcony, cocking his head to one side like a bird, and saw he couldn't climb up the rough but slick wall. The windows were closed with heavy iron shutters, and the massive iron door was locked. A sign hung from its handle. On it was a single word in the alphabet of the people of the northern continent of Kareen. SLEEPING.

Carmody shrugged, smiled indifferently, in contrast to his former wildness to get at the skin, and walked away. Abruptly the wind, which had died down, sprang into life again and struck him like a blow from a huge fist.

He rolled with it as he would have rolled with a punch in the ring, kept his footing, and leaned into it, head down but bright blue eyes looking upwards. Nobody ever caught him with his eyes shut.

There was a phone booth on the corner, a massive marble box that could hold twenty people easily. Carmody hesitated outside it but, impelled by the screaming fury of the wind, he entered. He went to one of the six phones and lifted its receiver. But he did not sit down on the broad stone bench, preferring to dance around, to shift nervously from side to side and to keep his head cocked as one eye looked for intruders.

He dialed his number, Mrs. Kri's boarding house. When she answered the phone, he said, "Beautiful, this is John Carmody. I want to speak to Father Skelder or Father Ralloux."

Mrs. Kri giggled, as he knew she would, and said, "Father Skelder is right here. Just a second."

There was a pause, then a man's deep voice. "Carmody? What is it?"

"Nothing to get alarmed about," said Carmody. "I think . . ."

He waited for a comment from the other end of the line. He smiled, thinking of Skelder standing there, wondering what was going on, unable to say too much because of Mrs. Kri's presence. He could see the monk's long face with its many wrinkles and high cheekbones and hollow cheeks and shiny bald pate, the lips like a crab's pincers tightening until they squeezed themselves out of sight.

"Listen, Skelder, I've something to tell you. It may or may not be important, but it is rather strange." He stopped again and waited, knowing that the monk was foaming un-

6

derneath that seemingly impassive exterior, that he would not care to display it at all and would hate himself for breaking down and asking Carmody what he had to tell. But he would break; he would ask. There was too much at stake.

"Well, well, what is it?" he finally snapped. "Can't you say over the phone?"

"Sure, but I wasn't going to bother if you weren't interested. Listen, about five minutes ago did anything strange happen to you or to anybody around you?"

There was another long pause, then Skelder said in a strained voice, "Yes. The sun seemed to flicker, to change color. I became dizzy and feverish. So did Mrs. Kri, and Father Ralloux."

Carmody waited until he was sure that the monk was not going to comment any further. "Was that all? Did nothing else happen to you or the others?"

"No. Why?"

Carmody told him about the skin of the unfinished face that had seemed to appear from the empty air before him. "I thought perhaps you might have had a similar experience."

"No; aside from the sick feeling, nothing happened."

Carmody thought he detected a huskiness in Skelder's voice. Well, he would find out later if the monk were concealing something. Meanwhile . . .

Suddenly, Skelder said, "Mrs. Kri has left the room. What is it you really wanted, Carmody?"

"I really wanted to compare notes about that flickering of the sun," he replied, crisply. "But I thought I'd tell you something of what I found out in the temple of Boonta."

"You ought to have found out just about everything," interrupted Skelder. "You were gone long enough. When you didn't show up last night, I thought that perhaps something had happened to you."

"You didn't call the police?"

"No, of course not," the monk's voice crackled. "Do you think that because I'm a priest I'm stupid? Besides, I hardly think you're worth worrying about."

Carmody chuckled. "Love thy fellow man as a brother. Well, I never cared much for my brother—or anybody else. Anyway, the reason I'm late, though only twenty hours or so behind time, is that I decided to take part in the big parade and the ceremonies that followed." He laughed again. "These Kareenans really enjoy their religion."

Skelder's voice was cold. "You took part in a temple orgy?"

Carmody hawhawed. "Sure. When in Rome, you know. However, it wasn't pure sensuality. Part of it was a very boring ritual, like all ritual; it wasn't until nightfall that the high priestess gave the signal for the mêlée."

"You took part?"

"Sure. With the high priestess herself. It's all right; these people don't have your attitude towards sex, Skelder; they don't think it's dirty or a sin; they regard it as a sacrament, a great gift from the goddess; what would seem to you infinitely disgusting, wallowing in a mire of screaming sex-fiends, is to them pure and chaste and goddess-blessed worship. Of course, I think your attitude and theirs are both wrong; sex is just a force that one ought to take advantage of in other people; but I will admit that the Kareenans' ideas are more fun than yours."

Skelder's voice was that of a slightly impatient and bored teacher lecturing a not-too-bright pupil. If he was angry, he managed to conceal it.

"You don't understand our doctrine. Sex is not in itself a dirty or sinful force. After all, it is the medium designed by God whereby the higher forms of life may be perpetuated. Sex in animals is as innocent as the drinking of water. And in the holy circle of matrimony a man and a woman may use this Godgiven force, may, through its sacred and tender rapture, become one, may approach that ecstasy, or be given an intimation of that ecstasy, which is the understanding and perhaps even glimpse of—"

"Jesus Christ!" said Carmody. "Spare me, spare me! What must your parishioners mutter under their breaths, what groans, every time you climb into the pulpit? God, or Whatever-it-is, help them!

"Anyway, I don't give a damn what the doctrine of the Church is. It's very evident that you yourself think that sex is dirty, even if it takes place within the permissible bonds of matrimony. It's disgusting, and the sooner the necessary evil is over and done with and one can take a shower, the better.

"However, I've gotten way off the track, which is that to the Kareenans these outbreaks of religio-sexual frenzy are manifestations of their gratitude to the Creator—I mean Creatrix—for being given life and the joys of life. Normally, they behave quite stuffily—"

"Look, Carmody, I don't need a lecture from you; after all, I am an anthropologist, I know perfectly well what the perverted outlook of these natives is, and—"

8

"Then why weren't you down here studying them?" said Carmody, still chuckling. "It's your anthropological duty. Why send me down? Were you afraid you'd get contaminated just watching? Or were you scared to death that you might get religion, too?"

"Let's drop the subject," said Skelder, emotionlessly. "I don't care to hear the depraved details; I just want to know if you found out anything pertinent to our mission."

Carmody had to smile at that word *mission*.

"Sure thing, Dad. The priestess said that the Goddess herself never appears except as a force in the bodies of her worshipers. But she maintains, as did a lot of the laymen I talked to, that the goddess's son, Yess, exists in the flesh, that they have seen and even talked to him. He will be in this city during the Sleep. The story is that he comes here because it was here that he was born and died and raised again."

"I know that," said the monk, exasperatedly. "Well, we shall see when we confront this impostor what he has to say. Ralloux is working on our recording equipment now so it'll be ready."

"OK," replied Carmody indifferently. "I'll be home within half an hour, provided I don't run across any interesting females. I doubt it; this city is dead—almost literally so."

He hung up the phone, smiling again at the look of intense disgust he could imagine on Skelder's face. The monk would be standing there for perhaps a minute in his black robes, his eyes closed, his lips working in silent prayer for the lost soul of John Carmody, then he would whirl and stalk upstairs to find Ralloux and tell him what had happened. Ralloux, clad in the maroon robe of the Order of St. Jairus, puffing on his pipe as he worked upon the recorders, would listen without much comment, would express neither disgust nor amusement over Carmody's behavior, would then say that it was too bad that they had to work with Carmody but that perhaps something good for Carmody, and for them, too, might come out of it. In the meantime, as there was nothing they could do to alter conditions on Dante's Joy or change Carmody's character, they might as well work with what they had.

As a matter of fact, thought Carmody, Skelder detested his fellow-scientist and co-religionist almost as much as he did Carmody. Ralloux belonged to an order that was very much suspect in the eyes of Skelder's older and far more conservative organization. Moreover, Ralloux had declared himself to be in favor of the adoption of the Statement of Historical Flexibility, or Evolution of Doctrine, the theory then being offered by certain parties within the Church, and advocated by them as worthy of being made dogma. So strong had the controversy become that the Church was held to be in danger of another Great Schism, and some authorities held that the next twenty-five years would see profound changes and perhaps a crucial break-up in the Church itself.

Though both monks made an effort to keep their intercourse on a polite level, Skelder had lost his temper once, when they were discussing the possibility of allowing priests to marry—a mere evolution of discipline, rather than doctrine. Thinking of Skelder's red face and roaring jeremiads, Carmody had to laugh. He himself had contributed to the monk's wrath by pointed comments now and then, hugely enjoying himself, contemptuous at the same time of a man who could get so concerned over such a thing. Couldn't the stupid ass see that life was just a big joke and that the only way to get through it was to share it with the Joker?

It was funny that the two monks, who hated each other's guts, and he, who was disliked by both of them and who was contemptuous of them, should be together in this project. "Crime makes strange bed-fellows," he had once said to Skelder in an effort to touch off the rage that always smoldered in the man's bony breast. His comment had failed of its purpose, for Skelder had icily replied that in this world the Church had to work with the tools at hand and Carmody, however foul, was the only one available. Nor did he think it a crime to expose the fraudulency of a false religion.

"Look, Skelder," Carmody had said, "you know that you and Ralloux were jointly commissioned by the Federation's Anthropological Society and by your Church to make a study of the so-called Night of Light on Dante's Joy and also, if possible, to interview Yess—providing he exists. But you've taken it on yourself to go further than that. You want to capture a god, inject him with chalarocheil and make him confess the whole hoax. Do you think that you won't get into trouble when you return to Earth?"

To which Skelder had replied that he was prepared to face any amount of trouble for this chance to kill the religion at its roots. The cult of Yess had spread from Dante's Joy to many a planet; its parody on the Church's ritual and Sacraments, plus the orgies to which it gave religious sanction had caused many defections from the Church's fold;

there was the fantastic but true story of the diocese of the planet of Comeonin. The bishop and every member of his flock, forty thousand, had become apostates and . . .

Remembering this, Carmody smiled again. He wondered what Skelder would say if he knew how literal his words were about "killing the religion at its root." John Carmody had his own interpretation of that. In his coat pocket he carried a True Blue Needlenose diminutive assassin, .03 caliber, capable of firing one hundred explosive bullets one after the other before needing a new clip. If Yess was flesh and blood and bone, then flesh could flower, blood could geyser, bone could splinter, and Yess would have another chance to rise again from the dead.

He'd like to see that. If he saw that, then he could believe anything.

Or could he? What if he did believe it? Then what? What difference would it make? So miracles were wrought? So what? What did that have to do with John Carmody, who existed outside miracles, who would never rise again from the dead, who was determined, therefore, to make the most of what little this universe had to offer?

A little of good food, steaks and onions, a little of good scotch, a little drunkenness so you could get a little closer but never close enough to the truth that you knew existed just on the other side of the walls of this hard universe, a little pleasure out of watching the pains and anxieties of other people and the stupid concerns they had over them when they could so easily be avoided, a little mockery, your greatest joy, actually, because it was only by laughing that you could tell the universe that you didn't care—not a false mockery, because he did not care, cared nothing for what others seemed to value so desperately—a little laughter, and then the big sleep. The last laugh would be had by the universe, but John Carmody wouldn't hear it, and so, you might say that he in reality had the last laugh, and . . .

At that moment he heard his name called by someone passing along the street. "Come on in, Tand!" Carmody shouted back in Kareenan. "I thought you'd gone to Sleep. You're not going to take the Chance, are you?"

Tand offered him a native-made cigarette, lit one of his own, blew smoke through narrow nostrils, and replied, "I've a very important deal to finish. It may take some time to complete it. So—I'll have to put off Sleeping as long as possible."

"That's strange," said Carmody, mentally noting that

11

Tand had answered him in terms as vague as possible. "I've heard that you Kareenans think only about ethics and the nature of the universe and improving your shining souls, not at all about dirty old money."

Tand smiled. "We are no different than most peoples. We have our saints, our sinners, and our in-betweens. But we do seem to have a Galaxy-wide reputation, though quite a contradictory one. One depicts us as a race of ascetic and holy men; the other, as the most sensual and vile of so-called civilized people. And, of course, strange stories are told about us, largely because of the Night of Light. Whenever we travel to another planet, we find ourselves treated as something quite unique. Which I suppose we are, just as all peoples are."

Carmody did not ask the nature of the important deal that was keeping Tand from going to Sleep at once. It would have been bad Kareenan form to do so. Over the glowing tip of his cigarette he studied him. The fellow was about six feet tall, handsome according to his own race's standards. Like most intelligent beings of the Galaxy, he could pass for a member of Homo Sapiens at a distance, his ancestors having evolved along lines parallel to those of Terrestrials. Only when he got closer could you see that his face, though manlike, was not quite human. And the feathery-looking hair and blue-tinged nails and teeth gave you a start when you first met a native of Dante's Joy.

Tand wore a gray, brimless, conical headpiece like a fool's cap, stuck jauntily onto one side; his hair was clipped quite close except just above the wolflike ears, where it fell straight down to cover them; his neck was encircled in a high lacy collar but his thigh-length, bright violet shirt was severe enough. A broad gray velvet belt gathered it in at the waist. His legs were bare, and his four-toed feet wore sandals.

Carmody had long suspected that the fellow was a member of the police force of this city of Rak. He always seemed to be around, and he had moved into the place that lodged Carmody the day after the Earthman had signed housepeace there.

Not that it mattered, thought Carmody. Even the police would be Sleeping in a day or so.

"What about yourself?" asked Tand. "Are you still insistent on taking the Chance?"

Carmody nodded and shot Tand a confident smile.

"What were you chasing?" added Tand.

Suddenly, Carmody's hands trembled, and he had to dig them in his pockets to hide them. His lips writhed in silent talk to himself.

Now, now, Carmody, none of this. You know nothing ever bothers you. But if that is so, why this shaking, this cold sickness in the dead center of your belly?

It was Tand's turn to smile, exposing his humanly shaped but blue-tinged teeth.

"I caught a glimpse of that thing you were chasing so desperately. It was the beginnings of a face, whether Kareenian or Terrestrial, I couldn't say. But since you doubtless conceived it, it must have been human."

"Wh-what d'ya mean, *conceived?* I, Conceived . . . ?"

"Oh, yes. You saw it form in the air in front of you, didn't you?"

"Impossible!"

"No, nor fantastic. The phenomenon, though not common, does occur now and then. Usually, a change takes place *in* the body of the conceiver, not outside. Your problem must be extraordinarily strong, if this thing takes place outside you."

"I have no problems I can't whip," growled Carmody out of one corner of his mouth, his cigarette bobbing from the other corner like a challenging rapier.

Tand shrugged. "Have it your own way. My only advice for you is to take a spaceship while there is still time. The last one leaves within four hours. After that, none will arrive or depart until the time for the Sleep is past. By then, who knows . . . ?"

Carmody wondered if Tand was being ironic, if he knew that he could not leave Dante's Joy, that he'd be arrested the moment he touched a Federation port.

He also wondered if Tand could have the slightest idea what he was planning as a means to leave Dante's Joy in full safety. Now, having regained full control of his hands, he took them from his pockets and removed the cigarette from his mouth. *Damn it,* he said, silently mouthing the words, *why are you hesitant, Carmody, old buddy? Lost your guts? No, not you. It's you against the universe, as it has always been, and you've never been afraid. You either attack a problem, and destroy it, or else ignore it. But this is so strange you can't seem to grapple with it. Well, so what? Wait until the strangeness wears off, then . . . BLAM! you've got it in your hands and you'll rip it apart, choke the life out of it, just as you did with—*

13

His hands clenched in memory of what they had done, and his lips stiffened into the beginning of a silent snarl. That face blowing through the air. Wasn't there a resemblance . . . could it have been . . . *No!*

"You are asking me to believe the impossible," he said. "I know that many strange things happen here on this planet, but what I saw, well, I just can't think that—"

"I have seen you Earthmen before when confronted by this," interrupted Tand. "To you it seems like something from one of your fairy-tales or myths. Or, perhaps, from that incredible phenomenon you call a nightmare, which we Kareenans do not experience."

"No," said Carmody. "Your nightmares occur outside you, every seven years. And even then most of you escape them by Sleeping, while we human beings can't encounter them except by means of sleeping."

He paused, smiled his rapid, cold smile, and added, "But I am different from most Earthmen. I do not dream; I have no nightmares."

"I understand," replied Tand evenly and apparently without malice, "that that is because you differ from most of them—and us—in that you have no conscience. Most Earthmen, unless I have been misinformed about them, would suffer troublings of the mind if they had killed their wives in cold blood."

The narrow walls of the booth thundered with Carmody's laughter. Tand looked emotionlessly at him until he had subsided into chuckling, then said, "You laugh loud enough but not nearly so loud as that."

He waved his hand to indicate the wind howling down the street.

Carmody did not understand what he meant. He was disappointed; he'd expected the usual violent reaction to his amusement at the subject of his "crime." Perhaps the fellow *was* a policeman. Otherwise, in the face of Carmody's laughter, how explain the stiff self-control? But it might be that he was untouched because the murder had happened on Earth and to a Terrestrial. An individual of one species found it difficult to get excited about the murder of a person belonging to another, especially if it was 10,000 light-years away.

However, there was the universally admitted deep empathy of the natives of Dante's Joy; they were acknowledged to be the most ethical beings in the world, the most sensitive.

Abruptly bored, Carmody said, "I'm going back to Mother Kri's. You coming along?"

"Why not? Tonight's the last supper she'll be serving for some time. She's going to Sleep immediately afterwards."

They walked down the street, silent for awhile though the wind, erratic as ever, had died down and made conversation possible. Around them towered the massive gargoyle-and-god-decorated buildings, built to last forever, to withstand any treatment from wind, fire, or cataclysm while their inmates slept. Here and there strode a lonely, silent native, intent on some business or other before he took the Sleep. The crowds of the day before were gone, and with them the noise, bustle, and sense of life.

Carmody was watching a young female cross the street and was thinking that if you put a sack on her head you wouldn't be able to distinguish her from a Terrestrial. There were the same long legs, the wide pelvis, seductive swaying of hips, narrow waist, and flowering of breasts . . . suddenly the light had changed color, had flickered. He looked up at the noonday sun. Blindingly white before, it was now an enormous disc of pale violet ringed by a dark red. He felt dizzy and hot, feverish, and the sun blurred and seemed to him to melt like a big ball of taffy, dripping slowly down the sky.

Then just as quickly as they had come, the dizziness and faintness were gone, the sun once again was an eye-searing white fire, and he had to look away from it.

"What the hell was *that?*" he said to no one in particular, forgetting that Tand was with him. He found out he was shivering with cold and was drained of his strength as if he'd been upended and decanted of half his blood.

"What in God's name?" he said again, hoarsely. Now he remembered that something like this had happened less than an hour ago, that the sun had changed to another color—violet? blue?—and that he'd been hot as if a fire had sprung up in his bowels and that everything had blurred. But the feeling had been much quicker, just a flash. And the air about three feet before him had seemed to harden, to become shiny, almost as if a mirror were forming from the molecules of air. Then, out of the seemingly much denser air, that face had appeared, that half-face, the first layer of skin, tissue-thin, whisked away at once by the wind.

He shivered. The wind's springing up again did not help his coolness. Then he yelled. About ten feet away from him, drifting along the ground, blown down the street and rolled

15

into a ball by now, was another piece of skin. He took a step forward, preparatory to running after it, then stopped. He shook his head, rubbed his long nose in seeming bewilderment, and unexpectedly grinned.

"This could get you down after a while," he said aloud. "But they're not getting their hooks into John Carmody. That skin or whatever it is can go floating on down into the sewer, where it belongs, for all I care."

He took out another cigarette, lit it, then looked for Tand. The native was in the middle of the street, bending over the girl. She was on her back, her legs and arms rigid but shaking, her eyes wide open and glazed, her mouth working as she chewed her lips and drooled blood and foam.

Carmody ran over, took one look, and said, "Convulsions. You're doing the right thing, Tand. Keep her from biting her tongue. Did you have medical training, too?"

He could have bit his own tongue then. Now the fellow would know a little more of his past. Not that it would help Tand much in gathering evidence about him, but he didn't like to reveal anything at all. Not without getting paid for it in one form or another. Never give anything away! It's against the laws of the universe; to keep living you have to take in as much or more than you put out.

"No, I didn't," replied Tand, not looking up but intent on seeing that the wadded handkerchief thrust into her mouth didn't choke her. "But my profession requires I learn a certain amount of first aid. Poor girl, she should have gone to Sleep a day earlier. But I suppose she didn't know she was liable to be affected this way. Or, perhaps, she did know and was taking the Chance so she might cure herself."

"What do you mean?"

Tand pointed at the sun. "When it discolors like that it seems to raise a tempest among one's brainwaves. Any epileptoid tendencies are revealed then. Provided the person is awake. Actually, though, you don't see this very often. Hereditary tendencies to such behavior have been nearly wiped out; those who gamble on the Chance usually are struck down, though not always. If one does come through, he is cured forever."

Carmody looked unbelievingly at the skies. "A flareup on the sun, eighty million miles away, can cause that?"

Tand shrugged and stood up. The girl had quit writhing and seemed to be peacefully asleep. "Why not? On your own planet, so I've been told, you are much influenced by solar storms and other fluctuations in the sun's radiations. Your people—like ours—have even charted the climactic, psychological, physical, business, political, sociological, and other cycles that are directly dependent upon changes on the surfaces of the sun, that can be predicted a century or more in advance. So why be surprised because our own sun does the same, though to a much more intense degree?"

Carmody began to make a gesture of bewilderment and helplessness, then halted his hand because he did not want anybody to think that he could for a moment be uncertain about anything.

"What is the explanation for all this—this hibernating, these incredible physiological transformations, this . . . this physical projection of mental images?"

"I wish I knew," said Tand. "Our astronomers have studied the phenomenon for thousands of years, and your own people have established a base upon an asteroid to examine it. However, after their first experience with the time of the Chance, the Terrestrials now abandon their base when the time for Sleep comes. Which makes it practically impossible to make a close examination. We have the same trouble. Our own scientists are too busy fighting their own psychical stress at this period to be able to make a study."

"Yes, but instruments aren't affected during these times."

Tand smiled his blue smile. "Aren't they? They register a wild hodgepodge of waves as if the machines themselves were epileptic. Perhaps these recordings may be very significant. But who can translate them? No one, so far."

He paused, then said, "That is wrong. There are three who could explain. But they won't."

Carmody followed the direction of his pointing finger and saw the bronze statuary group at the end of the street: the goddess Boonta protecting her son Yess from the attack of Algul, the dark god, his twin brother, in the metamorphosis of a dragon.

"Them . . . ?"

"Yes, them."

Carmody grinned mockingly and said, "I'm surprised to find an intelligent man like yourself subscribing to such a primitive belief."

"Intelligence has nothing at all to do with religious belief," replied Tand. He bent down over the girl, opened her eyelid, felt her pulse, then rose. He removed his hat with one hand and with the other made a circular sign.

"She's dead."

There was a delay of about fifteen minutes. Tand phoned

17

the hospital, and soon the long red oil-burning steam-driven ambulance rolled up. The driver jumped off the high seat over the front of the vehicle, which was built much like a landau, and said, "You're lucky. This will be our last call. We're taking the Sleep in the next hour."

Tand had gone through the girl's pockets and produced her papers of identification. Carmody noticed that he'd done so with a suspiciously policemanlike efficiency. Tand gave them to the ambulance men and told them that it would be best probably to wait until after the Sleep before notifying her parents.

Afterwards, as they walked down the street, Carmody said, "Who takes care of the fire department, the police work, the hospitals, the supplying of food?"

"Our fires don't amount to anything because of the construction of our buildings. Stocking food for seven days is no real problem; so few are up and out. As for the police, well, there is no law during this time. No human law, anyway."

"What about a cop who takes the Chance?"

"I said that the law is suspended then."

By then they'd walked out of the business district into the residential. Here the buildings did not stand shoulder to shoulder but were set in the middle of large yards. Plenty of breathing space. But the sense of massiveness, of overpoweringness, of eternity frozen in stone still hovered in the air, as these houses were every one at least three stories high and built of massive blocks and had heavy burglarproof iron doors and windows. Even the doghouses were built to withstand a siege.

It was seeing several of these that reminded Carmody of the sudden cessation of animal life. The birds that had filled the air with their cries the day before were gone; the lyan and kin, doglike and catlike pets, which were usually seen in large numbers even on the downtown streets, were gone. And the squirrels seemed to have retreated into the holes in their trees.

Tand, in reply to Carmody's remark about this, said, "Yes, animals instinctively sleep during the Night, have been doing it, from all evidences, since the birth of life here. Only man has lost the instinctive ability, only man has a choice or the knowledge of using drugs to put him in a state close to suspended animation. Apparently, even prehistoric man knew of the plant which gives the drug that will induce this sleep; there are cave paintings depicting the Sleep."

They stopped before the house belonging to the female

18

whom Carmody called Mother Kri. It was here that visiting Earthmen, willy-nilly, were quartered by the Kareenan government. It was a four-storied circular house built of limestone and mortar, capped by a thick shale roof, and set in a yard at least two hundred feet square.

A long winding tree-lined walk led up to the great porch, which itself ran completely around the house. Halfway up the walk, Tand paused beside a tree.

"See anything peculiar in this?" he asked the Earthman.

As was his habit when thinking, Carmody spoke aloud, not looking at his audience but staring off to one side as if he were talking to an invisible person. "It looks like a mature tree, yet it's rather short, about seven feet high. Something like a dwarf cottonwood. But it has a double trunk that joins about a third of the way up. And two main branches, instead of many. Almost as if it had arms and legs. If I were to come upon it on a dark night, I might think it was a tree just getting ready to take a walk."

"You're close," said Tand. "Feel the bark. Real bark, eh? It looks like it to the naked eye. But under the microscope, the cellular structure is rather peculiar. Neither like a man's nor a tree's. Yet like both. And why not?"

He paused, smiled enigmatically at Carmody, and said, "It is Mrs. Kri's husband."

Carmody replied coolly, "It is?" He laughed and said, "He's a rather sedentary character, isn't he?"

Tand raised his featherish eyebrows.

"Exactly. During his life as a man he preferred to sit around, to watch the birds, to read books of philosophy. Taciturn, he avoided most people. As a result he never got very far in his job, which he hated.

"Mrs. Kri had to earn money for them by starting this lodging house; she retaliated by making his life miserable with flagging him, but she could never fill him with her own enthusiasms and ambitions. Finally, partly in an endeavor to get away from her, I think, he took the Chance. And this is what happened. Most people said he failed. Well, I don't know. He got what he really wanted, his deepest wish."

He laughed softly. "Dante's Joy is the planet where you get what you really want. That is why it is off-limits to most of the Federation's people. It is dangerous to have your unconscious prayers answered in full and literal detail."

Carmody didn't understand everything he was being told, but he jauntily said, "Has anybody taken X-rays? Does he —it—have a brain?"

"Yes, of a sort, but what woody thoughts it thinks I wouldn't know."

Carmody laughed again. "Vegetable and/or man, eh? Look, Tand, what are you trying to do, scare me into getting off the planet or into taking the Sleep? Well, it won't work. Nothing frightens me, nothing at all."

Abruptly, his laughter ended in a choking sound, and he became rigid, staring straight ahead. His strength poured from him, and his body grew hot from his belly on out. About three feet before him there was a flickering like a heat wave, then, as if the air were solidifying into a mirror, the vibrations condensed into matter. Slowly, like a balloon collapsing as air poured out of holes torn in it, the bag of skin that had appeared folded in on itself.

But not before Carmody had recognized the face.

"Mary!"

It was some time before he could bring himself to touch the thing that lay on the sidewalk. For one thing, he didn't have the strength. Something had sucked it out of him.

Only his reluctance to display fear before somebody else moved him to pick it up.

"Real skin?" said Tand.

From someplace in the hollowness within him Carmody managed to conjure a laugh.

"Feels just like hers did, as soft, as unblemished. She had the most beautiful complexion in the world."

He frowned. "When it began to go bad . . ."

His fist opened out, and the skin dropped to the ground. "Empty as she was essentially empty. Nothing in the head. No guts."

"You're a cool one," said Tand. "Or shallow. Well, we shall see."

He picked up the bag and held it in both hands so it streamed out like a flag in the breeze. Carmody saw that there was now not only the face itself, but the scalp was complete and the front of the neck and part of the shoulders were there. Moreover, many long blond hairs floated like spider webs from the scalp, and the first layer of the eyeball itself had formed beneath the eyelids.

"You are beginning to get the hang of it," said Tand.

"I? I'm not doing that; I don't even know what's going on."

Tand touched his head and heart. "These know." He wadded the tissue in his fist and dropped it in a trashbasket on the porch.

"Ashes to ashes," said Carmody.

20

"We shall see," replied Tand again.

By this time scattered clouds had appeared, one of which masked the sun. The light that filtered through made everything gray, ghostly. Inside the house the effect was even worse. It was a group of phantoms that greeted them as they entered the dining room. Mother Kri, a Vegan named Aps, and two Earthmen, all sitting at a round table in a great darkened room flickeringly lit with seven candles set in a candelabrum. Behind the hostess was an altar and a stone carving of the Mother Goddess holding in her arms Yess and Algul as twin babies, Yess placidly sucking upon her right nipple, Algul biting down upon the left and scratching the breast with unbaby-like claws, the Mother Boonta regarding both impartially with a beatific smile. On the table itself, dominating the candelabrum and the plates and goblets, were the symbols of Boonta: the cornucopia, the flaming sword, the wheel.

Mother Kri, short, fat, large-bosomed, smiled at them. Her blue teeth looked black in the duskiness.

"Welcome, gentlemen. You are just in time for the Last Supper."

"The Last Supper," Carmody called on his way to the washroom. "Hah? I'll be my namesake, good old John. But who plays Judas?"

He heard Father Skelder snort with indignation and Father Ralloux's booming, "There's a little Judas in all of us."

Carmody could not resist stopping and saying, "Are you pregnant, too, dearie?" and then he walked away, laughing uproariously to himself. When he came back and sat down at the table, Carmody submitted with a smile to Skelder's saying grace and Mother Kri's asking for a blessing. It was easier to sit silent for a moment than to make trouble by insisting on the food being passed at once.

"When in Rome . . ." he said to Skelder and smiled to himself at the monk's puzzlement. "Pass the salt, please," he continued, "but don't spill it."

Then he burst into a roar of laughter as Skelder did exactly that. "Judas come back to life!"

The monk's face flushed, and he scowled. "With your attitude, Mr. Carmody, I doubt very much if you'll get through the Chance."

"Worry about yourself," said Carmody. "As for me, I intend to find some goodlooking female and concentrate so

21

much on her I'll not notice until long after that the seven days are up. You ought to try it, Prior."

Skelder tightened his lips. His long thin face was built for showing disapproval; the many deep lines in forehead and cheeks, the bony angles of cheek and jaw, the downward slant of the long meaty nose, the pattern of straight lines and whorls, these made up the blueprint of the stern judge, showed the fingerprints of a Maker who had squeezed out of this putty flesh an image of the righteous, then set the putty in a freezing blast to harden into stone.

The stone just now showed signs of being human, for it was distended and crimsoned with hot blood flooding beneath the skin. The pale blue-gray eyes glared from beneath pale gold eyebrows.

Father Ralloux's gentle voice fell like a benediction upon the room.

"Anger is not exactly one of the virtues."

He was a strange-looking man, this priest with his face made up of such contradictory features, the big pitcher-handle ears, red hair, pug nose, and broad smiling lips of the cartoon Irishman, all repudiated by the large dark eyes with their long feminine lashes. His shoulders were broad and his neck was thickly muscled, but his powerful arms ended in delicate and beautiful woman's hands. The soft liquid eyes looked gravely and honestly at you, yet you got the impression that there was something troubled in them.

Carmody had wondered why the fellow was Skelder's partner, for he was not at all well known, as the older man was. But he had learned that Ralloux had a fine reputation in anthropological circles. In fact, he was placed on a higher plane than his superior, but Skelder was in charge of the expedition because of his prominence in other fields. The lean monk was head of the conservative faction in the Church that was trying to reform the current morality of the laity; his taped image and voice had appeared upon every Federation planet that owned a caster; he had thundered forth a denunciation of nudity in the private home and on the public beach, of brief-contract marital relations, of polymorphous-perverse sexual attitudes, of all that had once been forbidden by Western Terrestrial society and especially by the Church but was now tolerated, if not condoned, among the laymen because it was socially acceptable. He wanted to use the Church's strongest weapons in enforcing a return to former standards; when the liberals and moderates in the Church accused him of being Victorian, he gladly adopted the title, declaring that that age was the one to which he desired they turn back. It was this background that was responsible now for the furious look he was giving Father Ralloux.

"Our Lord became angry when the occasion demanded! Remember the money-changers and the fig tree!" He pointed a long finger at his companion. "It is a misconception to think of Him as the gentle Jesus! One merely has to take the trouble to read the Gospels to perceive at once that He was a hard man in many respects, that—"

"My God, I'm hungry," said Carmody loudly, interjecting not only to stop the tirade but because he was famished. It seemed to him he'd never been so empty.

Tand said, "You'll find you'll have to eat enormous quantities of food during the next seven days. Your energy will be drained out as fast as it's put in."

Mother Kri went out of the room and quickly returned carrying a plate full of cakes. "There are seven pieces, gentlemen, each baked in the likeness of one of the Seven Fathers of Yess. These are always baked for certain religious feasts, one of which is the Last Supper before the Sleep. I hope you gentlemen do not mind partaking. A bit from each cake and a sip of wine with each is customary. This communion symbolizes not only that you are partaking of the flesh and blood of Yess but that you are given the power to create your own god, as the Seven did."

"Ralloux and I cannot do that," replied Skelder. "We would be committing a sacrilege."

Mrs. Kri looked disappointed but brightened when Carmody and Aps, the Vegan, said they would participate. Carmody thought it would be politic in case he wished to use Mrs. Kri later on.

"I do not think," said the woman, "that you would mind, Father Skelder, if you knew the story of the Seven."

"I do know," he said. "I made a study of your religion before I came here. I do not allow myself to remain ignorant on any subject if I can help it. As I understand it, the myth goes that in the beginning of time the goddess Boonta had two sons, self-conceived. Upon reaching manhood, one of the sons, the evil one, slew the other, cut him into seven pieces and buried them in widely separated places, so that his mother would not be able to gather them together and bring him back to life. The evil son, or Algul as you call him, ruled the world, restrained only by his mother from destroying humanity altogether. Wickedness was everywhere;

23

men were thoroughly rotten, as in the time of our Noah. Those few good people who did pray to the Mother to restore her good son, Yess, were told that if seven good men could be found in one place and at one time, her son would be resurrected. Volunteers came forth and tried to raise Yess, but never were enough qualified so that seven good men existed on this world at one time. Seven centuries went by and the world became more evil.

"Then, one day, seven men gathered together, seven *good* men, and Algul, the wicked son, in an effort to frustrate them, put everybody to sleep except seven of his most wicked worshippers. But the good seven fought off the Sleep, had a mystical union, a sort of psychical intercourse with the Mother"—Skelder's face twisted with distaste—"each of them becoming her lover, and the seven pieces of the son Yess were pulled together, reunited, and became alive. The evil seven turned into all sorts of monsters and the seven good became minor gods, consorts of the Mother. Yess restored the world to its former state. His twin brother was torn into seven pieces, and these were buried at different places over the earth. Since then, good has dominated evil, but there is still much evil left in the world, and the legend goes that if seven absolutely wicked men can gather together during the time of the Sleep, they will be able to resurrect Algul."

He paused, smiled as if in quiet mockery of this myth, then said, "There are other aspects, but that is the essence. Obviously, a symbolical story of the conflict between good and evil in this universe: many of its features are universal; they may be found in almost every religion of the Galaxy."

"Symbolism or not, universal or not," said Mrs. Kri, "the fact remains that seven men *did* create their god Yess. I know because I have seen him walking the streets of Kareen, have touched him, have seen him perform his miracles, though he does not like to do them. And I know that during the Sleep there are evil men who gather to create Algul. For they know that if he comes to life, then they, according to ancient promise, will rule this world and have all they desire."

"Oh, come now, Mrs. Kri. I do not want to decry your religion, but how do you *know* this man who claims to be Yess is he?" said Skelder. "And how could mere men fashion a god out of thin air?"

"I know because I know," she said, giving the age-old and unarguable answer of the believer. She touched her huge bosom. "Something in here tells me it is so."

Carmody gave his long, high-pitched irritating laughter.
"She's got you there, Skelder. Hoist by your own petard.
Isn't that the ultimate defense of your own Church when
every other has crumbled?"

"No," replied Skelder coldly, "it is not. For one thing, not
one of our so-called defenses crumbles. All remain rockfast,
impervious to the jeerings of petty atheists or the hammer-
blows of organized governments. The Church is imperishable,
and so are its teachings; its logic is irrefutable; the Truth is
its possession."

Carmody smirked but refused to talk any more about it.
After all, what difference did it make what Skelder or anybody else thought? The thing he wanted now was action;
he was tired of fruitless words.

Mrs. Kri had risen from the table and was clearing up
the dishes. Carmody, wishing to get more information out of
her, and also wanting the others unable to hear him, said that
he would help her clean up. Mrs. Kri was charmed; she
liked Carmody very much because he was always doing little
things for her and giving her little compliments now and
then. Astute enough to see that he had a purpose behind
this, she still liked what he did.

In the kitchen, he said, "Come on, Mother Kri, tell me
the truth. Have you actually *seen* Yess? Just as you've seen
me?"

She handed him a wet dish to dry.

"I've seen him more times than I have you. I had him in
for dinner once."

Carmody had difficulty swallowing this prosaic contact with
divinity. "Oh, really?"

"Really."

"And did he go to the bathroom afterwards?" he asked,
thinking that this was the ultimate test, the basic distinction
between man and god. You could think of a deity eating,
perhaps to render his presence easier to his worshippers,
perhaps also to enjoy the good things of life, but excretion
seemed so unnecessary, so un-divine that, well . . .

"Of course," said Mrs. Kri. "Does Yess not have blood
and bowels just as you and I?"

Skelder walked in at that moment, ostensibly for a drink
of water but actually, thought Carmody, to overhear them.

"Of course he does," the monk said. "Do not all men? Tell
me, Mrs. Kri, how long have you known Yess?"

"Since I was a child. I am fifty now."

"And he has not aged a bit, has always remained youthful,

25

untouched by time?" said Skelder, his voice tinged with sarcasm.

"Oh, no. He is an old man now. He may die at any time."

The Earthmen raised their eyebrows.

"Perhaps there is some misunderstanding here," said Skelder, speaking so swiftly as to give the impression of swooping down vulturelike upon Mrs. Kri. "Some difference in definition, or in language, perhaps. A god, as we understand the term, does not die."

Tand, who had come into the kitchen in time to catch the last few words, said, "Was not your god slain upon a cross?"

Skelder bit his lip, then smiled, and said, "I must ask you to forgive me. And I must confess that I have been guilty of a lapse of memory, guilty because I allowed a second of anger to cloud my thinking. I forgot for the moment the distinction between the Human and the Divine Nature of Christ. I was thinking in purely pagan terms, and even there I was wrong because the pagans' gods died. Perhaps you Kareenans made the same distinction between the human and the divine nature of your god Yess. I do not know. I have not been on this planet long enough to determine that; there was so much else to assimilate before I could study the finer points of your theology."

He stopped, sucked in a deep breath, then, as if he were getting ready to dive into the sea, he thrust his head forward, hunched his bony shoulders, and said, "I still think that there is a vast difference between your conception of Yess and ours of Christ. Christ was resurrected and then went to Heaven to rejoin His Father. Moreover, His death was necessary if He was to take on the sins of the world and save mankind."

"If Yess dies, he will someday be born again."

"You do not understand. There is the very important difference that—"

"That your story is true and ours false, a pagan myth?" replied Tand, smiling. "Who may say what is fact, what is myth, or whether or not a myth is not as much fact as, say, this table here? Whatever operates to bring about action in this world is fact, and if a myth engenders action, then is it not a fact? The words spoken here and now will die out in ever-weakening vibrations, but who knows what undying effect they may cause?"

Suddenly the room darkened, and everybody in it clutched for some hold, the top of a chair, the edge of a table, anything to keep oneself steady. Carmody felt that wave of heat sweep through him and saw the air before him harden, seeming to become glass.

Blood burst out of the mirror, shot as if from a hose nozzle into his face, blinded him, drenched him, filled his open mouth, drove its salty taste down his throat.

There was a scream, not from him but someone beside him. He jumped back, pulled his handkerchief out, wiped away the blood from his eyes, saw that the glassiness was gone and with it the spurt of blood, but that the table and the floor beside it were filmed in crimson. There must have been at least ten quarts of it, he thought, just what you would expect from a woman weighing one hundred pounds.

There was no chance to follow that up for he had to skip to one side to avoid Skelder and Mrs. Kri, who were wrestling across the kitchen, Mrs. Kri doing the pushing because she was heavier and, perhaps, stronger. Certainly, she was the more aggressive, for she was doing her best to strangle the monk. He was clutching at the hands around his neck and screaming, "Take your filthy hands off me, you . . . you *female!*"

Carmody roared with laughter, and the sound seemed to break the maniacal spell possessing Mrs. Kri. As if she were waking from a sleep, she stopped, blinked her eyes, dropped her hands, and said, "What was I doing?"

"You were choking the life out of me!" shouted Skelder. "What is the matter with you?"

"Oh, my," she said to no one in particular. "It's getting later than I thought. I'd better get to sleep at once. All at once it seemed to me that you were the most hateful man in the world, because of what you said about Yess, and I wanted to kill you. Really, I do get a little irked at what you say but not that much."

Tand said, "Apparently, your anger is much deeper than you thought, Mrs. Kri. You'd driven it into your unconscious, wouldn't admit it to yourself, and so—"

He didn't get to finish. She had turned to look at Carmody and had seen for the first time that blood covered him and was everywhere in the kitchen. She screamed.

"Shut your damn mouth!" said Carmody, quite passionlessly, and he struck her across the lips. She stopped screaming, blinked again, and said, in a quivering voice, "Well, I'd better clean up this mess. I'd hate to wake up and try to scrub off this stuff after it's dried. You're sure you're not hurt?"

He didn't answer her but instead walked out of the

kitchen and upstairs to his room, where he began to take off the wet clothing. Ralloux, who had followed him, said, "I am beginning to get scared. If such things can happen, and they obviously are not hallucinations, then who knows what will become of us?"

"I thought we had a little device that would make us quite safe?" said Carmody, peeling off the last of his sticky clothes and heading for the shower. "Or are you not sure of it?" He laughed at Ralloux's expression of despair and spoke from behind the veil of hot water hurtling over his head. "What's the matter? You really scared?"

"Yes, I am. Aren't you?"

"I, frightened? No, I have never been afraid of anything in my whole life. I'm not saying that to cover up, either. I don't really know what it is to feel fear."

"I strongly suspect you don't know what it is to feel *anything*," said Ralloux. "I wonder sometimes if you *do* have a soul. It must be there somewhere but thrust down so deep that nobody, including yourself, can see it. Otherwise . . ."

Carmody laughed and began soaping his hair.

"The headthumper at Johns Hopkins said I was a congenital psychopath, that I was born incapable of even understanding a moral code, I was beyond guilt, beyond virtue, not born with an illness of the mind, you understand, just lacking something, whatever it is that makes a human being human. He made no bones about telling me that I was one of those rare birds before which the science of the Year of Our Lord 2256 is completely helpless. He was sorry, he said, but I would have to be committed for the rest of my life, probably kept under mild sedation so I would be harmless and cooperative, and undoubtedly would be the subject of thousands of experiments in order to determine what it is that makes a constitutional psychopath."

Carmody paused, stepped from the shower, and began drying himself.

"Well," he continued, smiling, "you can see that I couldn't put up with that. Not John Carmody. So—I escaped from Hopkins, escaped from Earth itself, got to Springboard—on the edge of the Galaxy, farthest colonized planet of the Federation, stayed there a year, made a fortune smuggling sodompears, was almost caught by Raspold—you know, the galactic Sherlock Holmes—but eluded him and got here where the Federation has no jurisdiction. But I don't intend to stay here; not that it wouldn't be a bad world, because

28

I could make money here, too, the food and liquor are good, and the females are just unhuman enough to attract me. But I want to show Earth up for what it is, a stable for stupid asses. I intend to go back to Earth to live there in complete immunity from arrest. And to do pretty well what I please, though I shall be discreet about some things."

"If you think you can do that, you must be crazy. You would be arrested the moment you stepped off the ship."

Carmody laughed. "You think so? You know, don't you, that the Federal Anti-Social Bureau depends for its information and partly for its directives upon the Boojum?"

Ralloux nodded.

"Well, the Boojum after all is only a monster protein memory bank and probability computer. It has stored away in its cells all the available information about one John Carmody and it undoubtedly has issued orders that all ships leaving Dante's Joy should be searched for him. But what if proof comes that John Carmody is dead? Then the Boojum cancels all directives concerning Carmody, and it retires the information to mechanical files. Then, when a colonist from, say, Wildenwooly, who has made his pile there and wants to spend it on Earth, comes to the home planet, who is going to bother him, even if he does look remarkably like John Carmody?"

"But that's preposterous! In the first place, how is the Boojum going to get proof positive that you are dead? In the second place, when you land on Earth, your fingers, retina, and brainwaves will be printed and identified."

Carmody grinned joyfully. "I wouldn't care to tell you how I'll manage the first. As for the second, so what if my prints are filed? They won't be cross-checked; they'll just be those of some immigrant, who was born on a colony-planet and who is being recorded for the first time. I won't even bother to change my name."

"What if someone recognizes you?"

"In a world of ten billion population? I'll take my chance."

"What is to prevent my telling the authorities?"

"Do dead men tell?"

Ralloux paled but did not flinch. His expression was still the grave-faced gentle monk's, his large shining black eyes staring honestly at Carmody but giving him a slightly ludicrous appearance because of their unexpectedness in that snub-nosed freckled big-lipped pitcher-eared setting. He said, "Do you intend to kill me?"

Carmody laughed uproariously. "No, it won't be necessary.

29

Do you think for one moment either you or Skelder will come through the Night alive or in your right mind? You've seen what has happened during the few brief flickers we've had. Those were preludes, tunings up. What of the real Night?"

"What about what happened to you?" said Ralloux, still pale.

Carmody shrugged his shoulders, ran his hand through his blue-black porcupinelike hair, now clean of blood. "Apparently my unconscious or whatever you call it is projecting pieces of Mary's body, reconstructing the crime, you might say. How it can take a strictly subjective phenomenon and turn it into objective reality, I don't know. Tand says there are several theories that attempt to explain the whole thing scientifically, that leaves the supernatural out. It doesn't matter. It didn't bother me when I cut up Mary into little pieces, and it won't bother me to have pieces of her come floating back into my life. I could swim through her blood, or anybody else's, to reach my goal."

He paused, looked narrow-eyed but still grinning at Ralloux and said, "What did *you* see during those flickers?"

Ralloux, even paler, gulped. He made the sign of the cross. "I don't know why I should tell you. But I will. I was in Hell."

"In Hell?"

"Burning. With the other damned. With ninety-nine percent of all those who had lived, are living, and will live. Billions upon billions."

Sweat poured out of his face. "It was not something imagined. I *felt* the agony. Mine, and the others'.."

He fell silent, while Carmody cocked his head to one side like one puzzled bird trying to figure out another. Then Ralloux murmured, "Ninety-nine percent."

"So," Carmody said, "that is what you worry about most, that is the basic premise of your mind."

"If so, I did not know it," murmured the monk.

"How ridiculous can you get? Why, even your Church no longer insists upon the medieval conception of literal flames. Still, I don't know. From what I see of most people, they ought to fry. I'd like to be supervisor of the furnaces; there are some I've met in my short life whose fat egotism I'd like to burn right out of them. . . ."

Ralloux said, incredulously, *"You* resent egotists?"

Carmody, clean and dressed, grinned and started downstairs.

The mess, Mrs. Kri announced, was cleaned up and now she was going down into the vault to Sleep. She would leave the house open for their convenience, she said, but she hoped that when she awoke she wouldn't find everything too dirty, that they would wipe their feet before they came in and would empty the ashtrays and wash their dishes. Then she insisted upon giving each of them a peace-kiss, and broke down and cried, saying she might never see any of them again, and she asked Skelder's forgiveness for her attack upon him. He was quite gracious about it and gave her his blessing.

Five minutes later, Mrs. Kri, having injected herself with the necessary hibernatives, slammed the big iron door of the basement vault and locked herself in.

Tand bade them goodby. "If I'm caught before I get to my own vault, I'll have to go through the Night, willy-nilly. And once started, there's no holding back. It's all black and white then; you either get through or you don't. At the end of the seventh day, you are god, corpse, or monster."

"And what do you do with the monsters?" asked Carmody.

"Nothing, if they're harmless, like Mrs. Kri's husband. Otherwise, we kill them."

After a few more remarks, he shook hands, knowing this was an Earth custom, wishing them, not luck, but a suitable reward. He said goodby to Carmody last, holding his hand the longest and looking into his eyes. "This is your last chance ever to become anything. If the Night does not break up the frozen deeps of your soul, if you remain iceberg from top to bottom, as you now are, then you are done for. If there exists the least spark of warmth, of humanity, then let it burst into flame and consume you, no matter what the pain. The god Yess once said that if you would gain your life you must lose it. Nothing original in it—other gods, other prophets, everywhere there are sentient beings, have said so. But it is true in many ways, unimaginable ways."

As soon as Tand had left, the three Earthmen silently walked upstairs and took from a large trunk three helmets, each with a small box on its top, from which nodded a long antenna. These they put over their heads, then turned a dial just above the right ear.

Skelder smacked his thin lips doubtfully and said, "I certainly hope the scientists at Jung were correct in their theory. They said that the moment an electromagnetic wave is detected by this device, it will set up a canceling wave; that

31

no matter how vast the energies of the magnetic storm, we will be able to walk through them unaffected."

"I hope so," said Ralloux, looking downcast. "I see now that in thinking I could conquer what better men than I have found invincible, I was committing the worst sin of all, that of spiritual pride. May God forgive me. I thank Him for these helmets."

"I thank Him, too," said Skelder, "though I think that we should not have to have recourse to them. We two should put our full trust in Him and bare our heads, and our souls, to the evil forces of this heathen planet."

Carmody smiled cynically. "There is nothing holding you back. Go ahead. You might earn yourself a halo."

"I have my orders from my superiors," Skelder replied stiffly.

Ralloux rose and began pacing back and forth. "I don't understand it. How could magnetic storms, even if of unparalleled violence, excite the atomic nuclei of beings on a planet eighty million miles away, and at the same time probe and stir the unconscious mind, cause it to fasten an iron grip upon the conscious, provoke inconceivable psychosomatic changes? The sun turns violet, extends its invisible wand, rouses the image of the beast that lives in the dark caves of our minds, or else wakens the sleeping golden god. Well, I can understand some of that. Changes in electromagnetic frequencies on Earth's sun not only influence our climate and weather, they control human behavior. But how could this star act upon flesh and blood so that skin tension lessens, bones grow soft, bend, harden into alien shapes that are not found in the genes . . . ?"

"We still don't know enough about genes to say what shapes are implicit in them," interrupted Carmody. "When I was a medical student at Hopkins, I saw some very strange things." He fell silent, thinking about those days.

Skelder sat upright and thin-lipped on a chair, his helmet making him look more like a soldier than a monk.

"It won't be long," said Ralloux, still pacing, "before the Night will start. If what Tand says is true, the first twenty hours or so will put everybody who has stayed up—except us, who are protected by our helmets—into a deep coma. Seemingly, the bodies of the sleepers then build up a partial resistance so that they later wake up. Once awakened, they are so charged with energy or some sort of drive, that they cannot sleep until the sun is over its violent phase. It is while they are sleeping that we—"

"—shall do our dirty work!" said Carmody joyfully.

Skelder rose. "I protest! We are here on a scientific investigation, and we are allied with you only because there is certain work that we—"

"—don't want to soil our lily-white hands with," said Carmody.

At that moment the light in the room became dark, a heavy violet. There was dizziness, then a fading away of the senses. But it lasted only a second, though long enough to weaken their knees and send them crashing to the floor.

Carmody got up shakily on all fours, shook his head like a dog struck by a club, and said, "Wow, what a jolt that was! Good thing we had these helmets. They seem to have pulled us through."

He rose to his feet, his muscles aching and stiff. The room seemed to be hung with many violet veils, it was so dark and silent.

"Say, Ralloux, what's the matter with you?" he said.

Ralloux, white as a ghost, his face twisted with agony, leaped to his feet, screamed, tore the helmet off his head, and ran out the door. His footsteps could be heard pounding down the hall, down the steps. And the front door banged hard.

Carmody turned to the other monk. "He . . . now what's the matter with you?"

Skelder's mouth was open and he was staring at the clock on the wall. Suddenly, he whirled on Carmody. "Get away from me," he snarled.

Carmody blinked, then smiled and said, "Sure, why not? I never thought you had the skin I loved to touch, anyway."

He watched amusedly as Skelder began to edge along the wall towards the door. "Why are you limping?"

The monk did not reply but walked crabwise from the room. A moment later the front door banged again. Carmody, quite alone, stood a moment in thought, then examined the clock at which the monk had been staring. Like most Kareenian timepieces, it told the time of the day, the day, month, and year. The attack of violet had taken place at 17:25. It was now 17:30.

Five minutes had elapsed.

Plus twenty-four hours.

"No wonder my every muscle aches! And I'm so hungry!" Carmody said aloud. He took the helmet off and dropped it on the floor.

"Well, that's that. Noble experiment." He went downstairs into the kitchen, half-expecting to be struck in the face with more blood. But there was nothing untoward. Whistling to himself, he took food and milk from the refrigerator, made himself sandwiches, ate heartily, then checked the action of his gun. Satisfied, he rose and walked towards the front door.

The telephone rang.

He hesitated, then decided to answer it. Wothehell, he said to himself.

He lifted the receiver. "Hello!"

"John!" said a lovely female voice.

His head jerked away as if the receiver were a snake.

"John?" repeated the voice, now sounding far away, ghostly.

He sucked in a deep breath, squared his shoulders, resolutely put the phone to his ear again.

"John Carmody speaking. Who is this?"

There was no answer.

Slowly, he put the phone back on the hook.

When he left the house, he found himself in a darkness lit only by the streetlamps, islanded at hundred feet intervals, and by the huge moon, hanging dim and violet and malevolent above the horizon. The sky was clear, but the stars seemed far away, blobs straining to pierce the purplish haze. The buildings were like icebergs looming in a fog, threatening with their suddenness, seeming about to topple over. Only when he got close to them did they crystallize into stability.

The city lay silent. No bark of dog, no shrill of nighthawk, no toot of horn, no coughing, no slamming of door, no hard heels ringing on the sidewalk, no shout of laughter. If sight was muffled, sound was dead.

Carmody hesitated, wondering if he shouldn't commandeer a car he'd found parked by the curb. Four miles to the temple was a long walk when you thought about what might be roaming the violet-hazed darkness. Not that he was scared, but he didn't care for unnecessary obstacles. A car would give him speed for a getaway; on the other hand, it was much more noticeable.

Deciding he would ride it for the first two miles, then walk, he opened the door. He recoiled, and his hand grabbed for his gun. But it dropped. The occupant, lying face up on the seat, was dead. Carmody's flashlight, briefly turned upon the man's face, showed a mass of dried sores. Apparently, the driver had either been one who'd taken the Chance or else put off too long going to Sleep. Something, maybe an explosion of cancer, had eaten him up, had even

34

devoured the eyeballs and gulped away half of his nose.

Carmody pulled the body out and let it lie in the street. It took several minutes to get the water in the boiler heated up, then he drove off slowly, the headlights extinguished. As he cruised along, peering from side to side for strangers, keeping close to the curb on his left so he'd have contact with something solid, he kept thinking about the voice over the phone, trying to analyze how this thing could have come about.

To begin with, he thought, he must accept absolutely that he, John Carmody, through the power of his mind, out of the thin air, was creating something solid and objective. At least, he was the transmitter of energy. He didn't think his own body contained nearly enough power for the transmutation of energy into matter; if his own cells had to furnish it, they would burn up before the process was barely begun. Therefore, he must be, not the engine, but the transmitter, the transformer. The sun was supplying the energy; he, the blueprint.

Granted. So, if something he couldn't control—what a hateful but not to be denied thought!—if something he couldn't control was refashioning his dead wife, he at least was the engineer, the sculptor. What she was depended on him.

The only explanation he could find was that this process somehow utilized, not his conscious knowledge of the human body, but his body's unconscious self-knowledge. Through some means, his cells reproduced themselves directly in Mary's newly born body. Were the cells in her body, then, mirror-images, as the cells of one twin were of the other's?

That he could understand. But what about those organs that were peculiarly female? It was true that his memory contained a minute file on interior female anatomy. He'd dissected enough corpses; and as far as her own particular organs went, he knew those well enough, having taken her apart quite scientifically and carefully before feeding the pieces to the garbage disposal. He had even examined the four-months embryo, the prime cause of his anger and revulsion towards her, the swelling thing within her that was turning her from the most beautiful creature in the world to a huge-bellied monster, that would inevitably demand at least a small share of her love for John Carmody. Even a little bit was too much; he possessed the most precious, exquisite, absolutely unflawed thing of beauty; she was his, nobody else's.

And then, when he had proposed that they get rid of this flawing growth, and she had said no, and he had insisted, and had tried to force her, and she had fought him, then she had cried that she did not love him as she once had, that this child was not even his but that of a man who was a *man*, not a monster of egotism; then, for the first time in his life, as far as he remembered, he had been angry. Angry was an understatement. He had completely lost himself, had, literally, seen red, thought red, drowned in a crimson flood.

Well, that was the first, and last, time. He was here because of that time. Or was he? Even if he'd not gone insane with passion, wouldn't he have killed her anyway, later on, simply because logic would demand it? And simply because he could not stand the idea of the most beautiful being in the universe soiled and swollen, monstrous . . .

Maybe. It didn't matter what might have happened. What did happen was the only thing for a realist to consider.

There was the matter of her cells, which should be female but would not be if they were mirror-images of his. And there was the matter of her brain. Even if her body could be created female because of his knowledge of organs and of structure of genes, the brain would not be Mary's. Its original shaping, plus the billions of sub-microscopic groovings her memories would make, these would be beyond his power, conscious or unconscious.

No, if she had a brain, and she must have, then it would be his, John Carmody's, brain. And if his, then it must contain his memories, his attitudes. It would be bewildered at finding itself in Mary's body, would not know what to do, to think. But, being John Carmody, it would find a way to make the most of the situation.

He laughed at the thought. Why didn't he find her? He would then have the perfect woman, her flawless beauty plus his mind, which would agree absolutely with him. Sublime self-abuse.

Again he laughed. Mary had used that term herself in that last blazing moment before he went completely under. She had said that to him she was not a woman, a wife, but merely a superior instrument for making love to himself. She had never had that glorious feeling of being one flesh that should rightfully come to a loving and passionate wife, no, she had always felt alone. And she had had to go to another man, and then she had never really experienced the wonder of the two-made-one because she knew all the time that she was sinning and would have to cleanse herself through confession and repentance. Even that rightful sensation was spoiled for her. Nevertheless, she had felt more like a wife and a woman with this man than with her own husband.

Well, as he'd said, that was that. Dismiss the past. Think of the thing that looks like Mary.

(He was glad that this thing was taking place outside him, not in him, as it did with the others. Perhaps he did have a frozen soul, but if so, it was good to have one. The iciness repelled subjectivity, made the unconscious happen outside him, and he could deal with that, with a host of Marys, whereas he'd have been helpless if he'd been like that epileptic girl or Mrs. Kri's husband or the cancer-devoured owner of this car.)

Think of the thing that looks like Mary.

If she—it—was conceived out of your head, like Athena from Zeus's—then at the moment of birth she had, as far as you know, your mind. But from that moment on, she becomes an independent being, one with thoughts and motivations of her own. Now, John Carmody, if you somehow found yourself dispossessed of your native body, lodged in the flesh of a woman you had murdered, and knew at the same time that the other *you* was in your first body, what would you do?

"I", he said, murmuring to himself, "would accept at once the fact that I was where I was, that I could not get out. I would define the limitations I had to work within, and would then set to work. And what would I do? What would I want? I would want to get off Dante's Joy and go to Earth or some Federation planet, where I could easily find myself a rich husband, could insist on being his number one wife. Why not? I'd be the most beautiful woman in the world."

He chuckled at that thought. More than once he'd imagined himself as a woman, wondering what it would really be like, envious as far as it was possible for him to envy, because a lovely woman with his brain would have the universe by the tail, as tight a hold as you could get on the tail of this wildly bucking universe.

He'd—

And then his hands tightened on the steering wheel and he sat up straight as if the new idea had been a hot poker rammed into him.

"Why didn't I think of that sooner?" he said loudly. "My God, if she and I can come to some arrangement—and even if we can't, I'll find some way of forcing her—why, why, she is the perfect alibi! I never did confess that I killed her, not

37

to the authorities, anyway. And they never found the slightest trace of her. So, if I come back to Earth with her and say, 'Gentlemen, here is my wife. It's as I told you, she'd disappeared, and it turns out that she had an accident, was hit on the head, lost her memory, and somehow found her way to Dante's Joy . . . well, sure it sounds like a romantic novel, but remember such a thing does happen every now and then. What, you don't believe it? Well, gentlemen, take her fingerprints, photograph the pattern of blood vessels in her retina, type her blood, give her an EEG . . . Ah . . . !"

Ah, but wouldn't all those identification marks be John Carmody's if her cells were mirror-images of his? Possibly. But there was also the chance that she might have her own. He had seen the photographs of all of them, more than once, and while he couldn't consciously reproduce them, it might be that his unconscious, which presumably held an exact file of them, would have reconstructed them in this Mary-thing.

But the EEG. If that gray pulse in her skull were his . . .

Well, sometimes the pattern did change if the brain had been injured, and that disconcerting feature might be the thing to verify her story. But what about the zeta wave? That would indicate she was a male, and one glance from the authorities or anybody else would be enough to disprove that. Their next step would be to hold her for examination. The only time the zeta wave changed its rhythm from female to masculine or vice versa was when the subject changed sex. And examination would show that she was female, that her hormones were predominantly female. Or would it? If her cells were mirror-images of his, then the genes would be masculine, and perhaps the hormones, too. And what about an internal search? Would it expose female organs or would she internally be his duplicate?

For a second he was downcast, but his racing brain seized upon another alibi. Of course! She'd been on Dante's Joy during the seven days of the Chance, hadn't she? And that meant that she would probably undergo some strange change, didn't it? So, the discrepancies turned up in the laboratory, the brain waves, the hormones, even the contradictory internal organs, all these would be the result of her taking the Chance. She might attract considerable publicity, and she'd have to have a definite, unshakable story, but if she had his rigid will and iron nerves (and she would), then she'd stick it through and would demand her rights as a citizen of the Federation, and however reluctant, they'd have to allow her

38

her freedom. After that, what a team she and John Carmody would make!

If she were inclined to be cooperative, though, why hadn't she kept her telephone contact with him, arranged to meet him? If she had his brain, wouldn't she have thought of the same thing he had?

He frowned and whistled softly through his teeth. There was always one possibility he couldn't afford to ignore, even if he didn't like it. Perhaps she was *not* a female John Carmody.

Perhaps she *was* Mary.

He'd have to find out when he met her. In the meantime, his original plans were changed only slightly, to adjust to the realities of the situation. The gun in his coat pocket would still be used to give him the original, the unique, thrill he had promised himself.

At this moment he dimly saw, through the purplish halo cast by a streetlamp, a man and a woman. The woman was clothed, but the man was nude. They were locked in each other's arms, the woman leaning against the iron pillar of the lamp, forced back by the man's passionate strength. Forced? She was cooperating to the full.

Carmody laughed.

At that harsh sound, slapping the heavy silence of the night across the face, the man jerked his head upwards, gazed wide-eyed at the Earthman.

It was Skelder, but a Skelder scarcely recognizable. The long features seemed to have become even more elongated, the shaven skull had sprouted a light fuzz that looked golden even in this dark light, and the body, which had shed the monkish robes, showed a monstrous deformity of leg, a crookedness halfway between a man's limb and an animal's. Almost it was as if the bones had become flaccid and during the softness the legs had begun growing backwards. The naked feet themselves were extended from the legs so that he walked on tiptoe, like a ballerina, and they seemed to be covered with a light yellow shell that glistened like a hoof.

"The goat's foot!" said Carmody loudly, unable to restrain his delight.

Skelder loosed the woman and turned completely towards Carmody, revealing in his face the definitely caprine lines and in his body the satyr's abnormal yet fascinating repulsiveness.

Carmody threw back his head to laugh again, but stopped, his mouth open, suddenly choking.

The woman was Mary.

While he stared at her, paralyzed, she smiled at him, waved her hand gaily, then took Skelder's hand and started to walk off into the darkness with him, her hips swaying exaggeratedly in the age-old streetwalker's rhythm. The effect was, or would have been in other circumstances, half-comical, because of the six-months fat around waist and buttocks.

At the same time, Carmody was struck with a feeling he'd never had before, a melting heart-beating, wild sensation directed towards Skelder, mixed with a cold laughter at himself. He felt a terrible invincible longing for the monstrous priest but knew also that he was standing off to one corner and laughing sneeringly at himself. And underneath this was a slowly rising tide, threatening to overwhelm in time the other feelings, a not-to-be denied lust for Mary, tinged with a horror at himself for that lust and the strangeness of being ripped apart.

Against this host of invaders there was but one defense, and he took it immediately, springing out of the car, running around the hood, raising his gun, firing through the red mist that had replaced the purple.

Skelder, whinnying, threw himself to the ground and rolled over and over, a long bundle of gray-white laundry in the uncertain light, blown by the winds of desperation, disappearing in the darkness of the shadow of a tremendous flying buttress.

Mary whirled around, her open mouth a dark O in her pale face, her hands white birds imploring for mercy, then she dropped heavily.

And John Carmody staggered as he was struck one heavy blow after another in the chest and the stomach, felt his heart and viscera blasted apart, felt himself falling, falling, blood cascading all over him, falling into a darkness.

Someone had suddenly opened fire upon him, he thought, and this was the end and goodby and good riddance and the universe had the last laugh. . . .

And then he found he was awake, on his back, thinking these thoughts, staring straight up at the purple glove of the moon, a monstrous gauntlet flung into the sky by a monstrous knight. Come on, Sir John Carmody, fat little man clad in thin-skinned armor, enter the lists.

"Always game," he muttered to himself and rose unsteadily to his feet, his hands going unbelievingly over his body, groping for the great holes that he could have sworn were there. But they weren't; the flesh was unbroken, and his clothes were innocent of blood. Wet, yes, but with his sweat.

So that is how it is to die, he thought. It is horrible because it makes you feel so helpless, like a baby in the grip of an adult squeezing the life out of you, not because it hates you but because it must kill in the order of things, and squeezing is the only way it knows to carry out its order.

Stupefied at first, he was beginning to think clearly now. Obviously, those strange to-be-avoided-at-all-costs-even-to-losing-one's-temper sensations were those felt by Skelder and the Mary-thing, and the impact of the bullets tearing into her body had somehow been communicated to him, the shock so great that he'd lost consciousness or else his body had for that moment been fooled into thinking it was dead.

What if it had insisted on thinking so? Then he'd really be dead, wouldn't he?

Well, what of it?

"Don't fool yourself, Carmody," he said. "Whatever you do, don't fool yourself. You felt scared . . . to death. You called out for somebody to help you. Who? Mary? I don't think so, though it may have been. My mother? But her name is Mary. Well, it doesn't matter; the thing is that *I,* this thing up here," he said, tapping his skull, "was not responsible, it was John Carmody the child calling out, the youngster buried in me that used to cry for Mommy, in vain, because Mommy was usually out somewhere, working, or out with some man, anyway, always out, and I, I was alone and she wouldn't have come except to tell me what a little monster I was. . . ."

He walked over to Mary and turned her over.

A cry from the darkness made him jump. He whirled, his gun ready, but saw no one. "Skelder?" he called.

For answer he got another terrible cry, more like an animal's than a man's.

The street ran straight for a hundred yards ahead of him, then turned at a right angle. On the corner was a tall building, each of whose six stories overhung the one beneath, making it look like a telescope whose small end was stuck in the ground. Out of its shadows dashed Ralloux, his face twisted in agony. Seeing Carmody, he slowed to a walk.

"Stand to one side, John!" he cried. "You don't have to be in it, even if I do. Get out of it! I will take your place! I want to be in it! There's room for only one, and that space is reserved for me!"

"What the hell are you talking about?" growled Carmody. Warily, he kept his automatic pointed at the monk. No telling what maneuver this chaotic talk was supposed to cover up.

"Hell! I am talking about Hell. Don't you see that flame, feel it? It burns me when I am in it, and it burns others when I am not in it. Stand to one side, John, and let me relieve you of its pain. It will hold still long enough to consume me entirely, then, as I begin to adjust myself to it, it runs off and I must chase it down, because it settles around some other tortured soul and will not leave him unless I offer to dive into it again. And I do, no matter what the pain."

"You really are crazy," said Carmody. "You—"

And then he was screaming, had flung away his gun, was beating at his clothes, was rolling on the ground.

Just as suddenly as it had come, it was gone. He sat up, shaking, sobbing uncontrollably.

"God, I thought I was on fire!"

Ralloux had stepped forward onto the space occupied by Carmody and was standing there with his fists clenched and his eyes roaming desperately as if looking for some escape from his invisible prison. But seeing Carmody walking towards him, he fixed his gaze upon him and said, "Carmody, nobody deserves this, no matter how wicked! Not even you."

"That's nice," replied Carmody, but there was little of the old mocking tone in his voice. He knew now *what* the monk was suffering from. It was the *how* that bothered him. *How* could Ralloux project a subjective hallucination into another person, and make that person feel it as intensely as he did? The only thing he could think of was that the sun's curious action developed enormously in certain persons their ESP powers, or, if he discounted that, that it could transmit the neural activities of one person to another without direct contact. No mystery in that, certainly; it was within the known limitations of the universe. Radio transmitted sound, in a manner of speaking, just as TV did pictures; what you heard wasn't the original person, but the effect was the same, or just as good. However this was done, it was effective. He remembered now how he had felt in himself the bullets smashing into Mary, and had experienced the terror of death—whether it was his terror or Mary's didn't matter, and . . . would everybody he met during the seven nights transmit to him their feelings, and he be helpless to resist them?

42

No, not helpless; he could kill the authors of the emotions, the generators and broadcasters of this power.

"Carmody," shouted Ralloux, seemingly trying by the loudness of his voice to deafen the pain of the fire, "Carmody, you must understand that I do not have to stand in this flame. No, the flame does not follow me, I follow it and will not allow it to escape. I *want* to be in Hell.

"But you must not understand by that that I have lost my faith, have rejected my religion, and therefore have been flung headlong into the place where the flames are. No, I believe even more firmly in the teachings of the Church than before! I cannot disbelieve! But . . . I voluntarily have consigned myself to the flame, for I cannot believe that it is right to doom ninety-nine percent of God-created souls to hell. Or, if it is right, then I will be among the wrong.

"Believing absolutely every iota of the Creed, I still refuse to go to my rightful place among the blest, if such a place was ever reserved for me! No, Carmody, I range myself among the eternally damned, as a protest against divine injustice. If a fraction only are to be spared, or even if things were reversed, and ninety-nine point nine nine nine to the ninety-ninth place souls were to be saved, and one solitary soul were to have Hell all to itself, I should renounce Heaven and stand in the flames with that piteous soul, and I should say, 'Brother, you are not alone, for I am here with you to eternity or until God relents.' But you would not hear one word of blasphemy from me, nor one word of pleading for mercy. I should stand and burn until that one soul were freed of its torment and could go to join the ninety-nine point nine nine nine to the ninety-ninth place. I . . ."

"Raving mad," said Carmody, but he was not so sure. Though Ralloux's face was contorted in agony, the look of dissonance, the splitting effect, as of two warring forces, was gone. He now appeared, though in pain, to be at one with himself. Whatever it was that had seemed to tear him apart from within was gone.

Carmody could not think of what it was that could cause the cleavage to vanish, especially now when, under the circumstances, he would have thought it'd be even more stressed. Shrugging, he turned to walk back towards the car. Ralloux yelled something else, something warning yet at the same time entreating. The next second, Carmody felt that terrible searing heat at his back; his clothes seemed to smoke and his flesh gave a silent scream.

43

He whirled, firing his gun in the general direction of the monk, unable to see him because of the glare of flame.

Suddenly, the dazzling light and the scorching heat were whisked away. Carmody blinked, readjusting his eyes to the dim purple, looking for Ralloux's body, thinking that the hallucination must have died with the projector of it. But there was only one corpse, Mary's.

Down the street, something black-looking slipped around the corner. A scream drifted back. Ralloux in hot pursuit of his torture and justification.

"Let him go," said Carmody, "as long as he takes the flame with him." But, he thought, it was the flame that was dragging the monk after it.

Now that Mary was dead, it was time to determine for himself something about which he'd wondered very much.

It took him a little while. He had to get out of the car's toolbox a hammer and a dull chisel-like instrument that was probably used to pry the hub cap and the tire from the wheel. With these he managed to split her skull open. Putting the tools down, he picked up the flashlight and on his knees bent over close to the open cranium, holding his coat over him to give some cover for the beam. He pressed the light's button, shining it straight into the hole, his face close as possible to the brain. It was not, he knew, that he would be able to distinguish between a man's brain, his, and a woman's brain, Mary's. But he was curious to see if she did have a brain or if, perhaps, there was just a large knot of nerves, a nexus for the telepathic orders that he gave it. If her life and her behavior were somehow dependent upon the workings of his own unconscious, then . . .

The light sprang into being.

There was no brain that he could see. Just what it was he had no time then to determine, only time to see a coiled shape, glittering red eyes, a gaping white-fanged mouth, and then a blur as it struck.

He fell back, the light falling from his hand and rolling away, its beam shining out into the night. He didn't care or even think about it, for his face had begun puffing up at once. It was like a balloon, swelling as if air were being pumped into it at a very fast rate. And at the same time, an intense pain spread from it, ran down his neck and into his veins. Fire invaded his body, spreading through him as if his blood were turning into molten silver.

There was no running away from this flame, as there had been from Ralloux's.

He screamed again and again, leaped to his feet, and, half out of his mind, drove his heel in hysterical fury and pain against the snake whose fangs had bitten into his cheek and whose tail merged into the cluster of nerves at the base of Mary's spine, growing from it. It had been living coiled up in her skull, surely waiting for the time when John Carmody would open its bony nest. And it had released its deadly poison into the flesh of the man who had created it.

Not until the horrible thing had been crushed beneath his heel, smashed into a blob from which two long curved broken fangs still stuck out, did Carmody cease. Then he fell to the ground beside Mary, the tissue of his body seeming like dry wood that had burst into flame, and the terror of dissolving forever wrenching a choked cry from a throat that had seemed too full of a roaring fear to utter ever again. . . .

There was one thought, the only shape in the chaos, the only cool thing in the fire. He had killed himself.

Somewhere in the moon-tinged purple mist a bell was ringing.

Far off, the referee was chanting slowly, ". . . *five, six, seven . . ."*

Somebody in the crowd—Mary?—was screaming, "Get up, Johnny, get up! You've got to win, Johnny boy, get up, knock that big brute down! Don't let him count you out, Joh-oh-oh-oh-neeee!"

"Eight!"

John Carmody groaned, sat up and tried, in vain, to get on his feet.

"Nine!"

The bell was still ringing. Why should he get up when he was saved by the bell?

But then why hadn't the ref quit counting?

What kind of a fight was this where the round wasn't over even if the bell did ring?

Or was it announcing the opening of a new round, not the closing of an old?

"Gotta get up. Fight. Whale hell outa that big bastard," he muttered.

"Nine" still hung in the air, as if it had yelled in the mist and was glowing there, faintly, violently phosphorescent.

Who was he fighting? he asked, and he rose, shakily, his eyes opening for the first time, his body crouching, his left fist sticking out, probing, his chin behind his left shoulder, his right hand held cocked, the right that had once won him the welterweight championship.

But there was no one there to fight. No referee. No crowd. No Mary screaming encouragement. Only himself.

Somewhere, though, there *was* a bell ringing.

"Telephone," he muttered, and looked around. The sound came from the massive granite public phone booth half a block away. Automatically, he began walking towards it, noticing at the same time what a headache he had and how stiff his muscles were and how his guts writhed uneasily within him, like sleepy snakes being awakened by the heat of the morning sun.

He lifted the receiver. "Hello," he said, at the same time wondering why he was answering, knowing that it couldn't possibly be for him.

"John?" said Mary's voice.

The receiver fell, swung, then it and the phone box erupted into many fragments as Carmody emptied a clip at them. Pieces of the red plastic struck him in the face, and blood, real blood, his, trickled down his cheeks and dripped off his chin and made warm channels down the sides of his neck.

Stiffly, almost falling, he ran away, reloading his gun but saying over and over, "You stupid fool, you might have blinded yourself, killed yourself, stupid fool, stupid fool. To lose your head like that."

Suddenly, he stopped, put the gun back into his pocket, took out a handkerchief, and wiped the blood off his face. The wounds, though many, were only surface-deep. And his face was no longer swollen.

Not until then did he perceive the full significance of the voice.

"Holy Mother of God!" he moaned.

Even in his distress, one part of him stood off, cool observer, and commented that he'd not sworn since childhood, but now he was on Dante's Joy he seemed to be doing it at every turn. He had long ago given up using any blasphemous terms because, in the first place, almost everybody did, and he didn't want to be like everybody, and, in the second place, if you blasphemed, you showed you believed in what you were blaspheming against, and he certainly didn't believe.

The cool observer said, "Come on, John, get a grip on yourself. You're letting this shake you. We don't let anything shake us, do we?"

He tried to laugh, but succeeded only in bringing out a croak, and it sounded so horrible that he quit.

"But I killed her," he whispered to himself.

"Twice," he said.

He straightened up, put his hand in his pocket, gripped the gun's butt tightly. "OK, OK, so she can come back to life, so I'm responsible for it, too. So what? She can be killed, again and again, and when the seven nights are up, then she's done forever, and I'll be rid of her forever. So, if I have to litter this city from one end to the other with her corpses, I'll do it. Of course, there'll be a tremendous stink afterwards"—he managed a feeble laugh—"but I won't have to clean up the mess, let the garbage departments do that."

He went back to the car but decided first to look at the old body of Mary.

There were huge pools of black blood on the pavement and bloody footprints leading off into the night, but the dead woman was gone.

"Well, why not?" he whispered to himself. "If your mind can produce flesh and blood and bone from the thin air, why can't it even more easily repair blasted flesh and blood and bone and re-spark the dead body? After all, that's the Principle of Least Resistance, the economy of Nature, Occam's razor, the Law of Minimum Effort. No miracles in this, John, old partner. And everything's taking place outside you, John. The inner you is secure, unchanged."

He got into the car and drove on. Because the night seemed a little brighter, he drove a little faster. His mind, too, seemed to be coming out of the slowness induced in it by the recent shocks, and he was thinking with his former quick fluidity.

"I say, 'Arise from the dead,' and they arise," he said, "like Jairus' daughter. *Talitha cumi.* Am I not a god? If I could do this on some other planet, I would *be* a god. But here," he added, chuckling with some of his old vigor, "here I am just a bum, one of the boys, prowling the night with the other monsters."

The avenue ahead of him drove straight as a kaser beam for two kilometers. Normally, he would have been able to see the Temple of Boonta at the end of the avenue. But now, despite the enormous globe of the moon, halfway up the sky, he could discern the structure only as a darker purple bulk looming in the lesser purple. The mass gave only a hint that it was formed of stone and not of shade,

47

that it was itself the substance and not the shadow. And the hint was ominous.

Above it, the moon shone golden-purple in the center and silver-purple around the edges. So huge was it, it seemed to be falling, and this apparent down-hurtling was strengthened by the slight shifting of hue in the purple haze. When Carmody looked directly at the moon, it billowed. When he looked to one side, the moon shrank.

He decided to quit staring through the windshield at the uncertain globe. Now was no time to get lost in the monster, to feel utterly small and helpless beneath its overbearing bulk. It was dangerous to concentrate on anything in this darkness of threats. Everything seemed ready to swallow him up. He was a little mouse in the midst of giant purple cats, and he did not like the feeling.

He shook his head as if trying to waken himself, which was, he thought, exactly correct. Those few seconds of looking at the moon had almost put him to sleep. Or, at least, the brief time had sucked much awareness from him. The moon was a purple sponge that absorbed much—far too much. He was now only a half a kilometer from the Temple of Boonta, and he did not remember traveling the last kilometer and a half.

"Whoa, John!" he muttered. "Things are going too fast!"

He steered the car to the base of a statue in the middle of the avenue. The vehicle would be hidden by the broad base from the view of anyone who might be standing before the Temple. Also, it would be concealed from anyone inside the Temple itself and looking out its windows.

He got out of the car and peered around the base. As far as he could see—a limited distance in these purplish veils—there were no living beings. Here and there a few bodies on the pavement and a few more sprawled on the ramp that led to the great portico of the Temple. But there was nothing dangerous. Not, that is, unless someone was playing possum, hoping that a careless passerby would not dream that the motionless body, apparently slain, would leap up to become the slayer.

Cautiously, he approached. Before getting close to any of the bodies, he stopped to watch them. None gave any sign of life. Indeed, most of them could not possibly be living. They were torn apart or else so mutilated or disfigured by growths or distortions, they could not have survived.

He passed the bodies and walked up to the ramp. The dark stone pillars of the portico soared, their upper parts dim in the coiling haze. The lower parts were carved into the shapes of great legs. Some were male, some female.

Beyond the vast legs was shadow—shadow and silence. Where were the priests and priestesses, the choir, the image-bearers, the screaming women red from head to foot with their own blood, shaking the knives with which they had slashed themselves? Earlier—how much earlier?—when he had attended the rituals, he had been one man lost in thousands, in a crashing noise. Now, darkness and a singing silence.

Did the god Yess live in the Temple, as every Kareenan to whom he had talked had insisted? Was Yess even now in the Temple and waiting for another Night of Light to pass? The story was that Yess could never be sure, during this time, that his Mother would not withdraw Her grace from him. If Algul won, then Algul, or one of his followers rather, would kill Yess. Sometimes, so the myth said, a follower of Algul would be so strong—so great with evil—he would be able to kill the god Yess.

Then, when the Night ended, and the Sleepers awakened, a new god would be reigning. And the worshipers of Algul would have their way until the next Night began.

John Carmody's heart beat even faster. What greater act than to kill a god? Decide! Now, that was something only one man among many billions could boast of being. A deicide. And if his reputation had been high before, known throughout the Galaxy, think of what it could become. His stealing of the Starinof Shootfire was nothing compared to this! Nothing!

Up to now, he told himself, he had done nothing. He gripped his gun barrel, then relaxed his hold because it was too tight. He walked between the ankles of a stone woman. The purple thickened into black, but he walked slow step by step forward. Ahead, he could see nothing. Once, he turned to look back. There was light, or at least some illumination, a cerulean glow between the legs of the statues. Beyond this, the dark did not seem to intensify. Instead, the light wavered, like a sheet rippled by wind.

He turned around to face the darkness across the Temple face. He did not know what the wavering of light meant, but it had managed to threaten something that outweighed all the many threats he had encountered during this long Night.

Or was it something projected by someone to force him to go into the Temple?

49

He paused. He did not at all like the idea that something knew he was here, was waiting for him, and was eager to get hold of him.

He murmured, "Don't be getting spooked now, John. When in hell before did you ever get so nervous? So, why now? Even if this is the Big One, don't let it get to you. You can't afford to let it. Besides, what the hell's the difference, one way or the other? Either you make it or you don't.

"Still, I'd like to do it. Show those other bastards."

He did not know what he meant by his last remark nor did he reflect on it. Was there anything wrong in wanting to outdo all the others? Maybe. He should not care.

He thrust the idea away. The business here and now had to be taken care of. Despatched . . . no, dispatched. Both.

Suddenly, without any sensory indication, he knew he had passed from the portico into the Temple interior. There was neither lessening nor increasing of light or of sound. But he knew he was inside. Without being able to see it, he could visualize the floor of polished medium-red stone stretching at least half a kilometer from entrance to farther wall. The sides of the room would also be glass-smooth. They would bend imperceptibly, curving gently inward to form a sphere. Unlike the exterior architecture, stone almost drunken with image, the interior walls were bare as the shell of an egg.

Slowly, he walked forward. His knees were slightly bent; he was ready to spring away at the smallest sound or merest touch. The darkness was congealing around him. It felt thick, as if it were pouring into his ears and eyes and nostrils and making the blackness inside him even denser. When he turned so he could keep track of the direction by which he had entered, he could no longer see the outline of the archway. He was a mote of dust in a beam of unlight.

But he was not floating; he had free will. He was driven by no one but himself, and he had a goal.

Even so, he was taking a long time to get there. Step by step over half a kilometer, with frequent pauses to listen, took time. Finally, when he was wondering if he were not angling off, his toe touched something solid. He knelt to feel with his hand. It was the primary slab. He lifted his foot, stepped up on the rock, and advanced. The second slab stopped his cautious foot. He stepped upon that and shuffled on until he came to the throne.

"Let's see," he mumbled. "The chair faces this way, towards the entrance. So, if I go in a straight line from the back of the chair, I come to the little entrance at the wall. And beyond that . . ."

Beyond that wall, he had been told, was the Arga Uboonota, the Holy of Holies. To get to it, one pushed on the wall, and a door of stone swung inward. The chamber to which the door gave access was supposed to be one into which only the elect of the elect were admitted. These would be the higher priests and priestesses, the great statesmen, and, of course, the arrshkiim. This Kareenan word could be translated as "the passed": those who had survived the Night of Light.

In that chamber the higher mysteries were celebrated. Also in this room, if he could believe the Kareenans, were born the gods Yess and Algul. In this room, the Great Goddess Boonta sometimes made Her presence known. And here she communed mystically with the Good Seven or the Evil Seven to procreate Her sons.

The door itself, so he understood, was never locked. No Kareenan who did not think himself worthy would dare to open it or even to look inside if it were accidentally opened. And the elect passed through at extreme peril.

"Boonta doesn't care what She eats, and She is often hungry," was a Kareenan proverb. The speaker never elaborated, perhaps because he knew no more than the saying itself and had never considered the implications. Perhaps he was afraid to consider them. But the speaker always made that circular sign during the utterance, as if he were protecting himself.

John Carmody had been convinced that the Kareenan religion was based on a fraud that used superstition to advance itself, as all religions did. Now he was not so sure there were not some genuine elements in Boontism. Too many events that would be unbelievable elsewhere had actually occurred here.

His outstretched right hand, the free one, touched the wall. The stone felt warm, too warm. It was as if there were a fire on the other side.

He pushed, and the wall gave. The door was swinging in. No light streamed through. It was as dark within as without.

For a long time he stood with his hand on the wall door, unwilling to go in and unwilling to stay. If he entered and let the door swing shut, he might be trapped.

"What the hell!" he murmured. "All or nothing."

He pushed harder as he entered, and the door moved without a sound. Although he kept his hand close to it, or tried to do so, he could not feel a displacement of air as it closed. But closed it was, with no way he knew to open it. He tried, but it did not budge.

For a moment, he thought of using his flashlight. He might be able to detect anyone moving in on him, surprise him, get in the first blow. But, if his presence was not known, he would be a fool to give it away. No, he would move about in the darkness that had always been his ally. He was the cat; other men, the mice.

Slowly, he stepped forward, pausing every three paces to listen. The silence droned. He could hear the thrum of blood in his ears and even, he thought, the beat of his heart.

Or was it *his* heart?

There was a *thum-thum* as of drumsticks wrapped in wool tapping on a faroff drum. Yet, something about the strokes felt close, close enough to be echoes from a heart close to his.

He turned slowly, trying to locate the origin of the sound. Or was it a phantom of sound? Or could it be some type of engine turning lazily over, or a piston stroking slightly out of phase with that engine inside his own breast?

Maybe, he thought, this chamber has a resonance which detects, amplifies and reprojects the noise of the slow convulsions of my heart.

No, that was absurd.

Then, by God, what was it?

The air was creeping over him, cooling him as it passed over the sweat on his face. The temperature of the room itself was neither too warm nor too cold. But he was perspiring as if in a hot place, and at the same time he was shaking as if it were cold. Moreover, he now smelled an odor such as he had never experienced before. It was the odor of ancient stone; somehow, he knew its identity.

He swore soundlessly and forced himself to stop quivering. He succeeded, but now the air itself seemed to quiver.

Was this the physical equivalent of the physical manifestations that had taken place several times before? The times when the air had seemed to harden, to shimmer as if turning into a glassy jelly? Was Mary forming again before him? In this darkness?

He glared and opened his mouth in a snarl.

I'll kill her, he thought. Kill! There'll be nothing left of her —nothing but bloody gobbets. I'll destroy her so thoroughly, she'll never come back again.

Not caring what might result from giving himself away,

he took the flashlight from the pocket in his cloak. The beam thrust out across a vast expanse, and then its circle fell upon the wall at the other end. Stone with dark-red veins spiraling across a fleshy white.

He traveled the beam across the huge room. He stopped. A stone statue reared toward the ceiling. It was fully sixty meters high, a titanic woman, naked, with many swollen breasts. One hand was in the act of pulling a squawling baby from her womb. The other hand was clutched around a second infant. This one was squawking soundlessly with terror, for the woman's mouth was open—her fanged mouth—and she was about to bite down upon the head of the infant.

Other babies were sprawled about her body. Some were mouthing her nipples. Some were falling from her breasts, caught stonily in their failure to keep hold of and get nourishment from the mountain-slope teats.

The face of the goddess Boonta was a study in split personality. One eye, fixed on the baby about to be devoured, was wild and savage. The other eye was half-lidded, calm, maternal, bent upon a baby feeding contentedly on the nearest breast. One side of the face was loving, the other vicious.

"OK," John Carmody muttered. "I get the message. So this is the great Boonta. A stinking idol of a stinking bunch of stinking barbarians."

His beam swept down. Clutching each leg was a stone child, each about five years old, if their proportions as compared to Boonta's meant anything. Yess and Algul, he supposed. Both were looking up at her with expressions of hopeful fear or fearful hope.

"A lot of motherly love you'll get out of her," he said. "About as much as I got from my mother—the bitch!"

At least, he thought, his mother had not materialized out of the air. Too bad. He would have taken almost as much pleasure blowing her guts out as he had the materialization of Mary.

He continued to sweep the beam around. It stopped when it illuminated an altar of stone half-covered with a velvety wine-red cloth. On top of the altar, in the middle, was a massive golden candleholder. It had a round base and a thick pedestal with a golden snake coiled just below the space for the candle. The candle, however, was missing.

"I'm eating it," a Kareenan male said.

Carmody whirled, and almost pulled the trigger of his

automatic. His flashlight spotlighted the man, who was sitting on a chair. He was large and well built. His face was, by Kareenan and even by human standards, handsome.

But he was old. The blue feathery hairs on his head were white, as were the pubic hairs. He had many wrinkles on his face and neck.

The Kareenan took another bite from the half-eaten candle. His jaws moved vigorously while his blue eyes remained fixed on Carmody. The Earthman stopped when he was a few feet from him. He said, "The great god Yess, I presume?"

"I know the reference in the phrase," the Kareenan said. "You are a cool one. To answer your question, I am Yess. But not for long."

Carmody decided the Kareenan was no immediate threat. He continued his examination of the room by flashlight. At one end was an archway with steps leading upward. Above, projecting from the wall at a height of about forty meters, was a balcony. It was capable of holding about fifty spectators on its banked array of seats. The wall at the other end had a similar archway and balcony. That was all. The room contained only the gigantic statue of Boonta, the altar and candleholder, the chair, and the man—god?—in it.

Yess, or a decoy?

"I am truly Yess," the Kareenan said.

Carmody was startled.

"Can you read my mind?"

"Don't get so panicky. No, I cannot read your mind. But I can perceive your intentions."

Yess swallowed the bite. After sighing, he said, "The Sleep of my people is troubled. They are having a nightmare. Monsters are thrusting upward from the depths of their beings. Otherwise, you would not be here. Who knows what this night will see? Perhaps . . . the time for Algul to triumph? He is impatient with his long exile." He made the circular sign. "If Mother so wills it."

"My curiosity will be the death of me yet," Carmody said. He laughed but cut the laugh off when the cachinnations were hurled back at him from the far-off walls.

"What do you mean by that?" Yess asked.

"Not much," Carmody replied. He was thinking that he should kill this man—god—while he had the chance. If Yess' retainers appeared, they could make it unhealthy for the man who intended to assassinate their god. On the other hand, what if this Kareenan was not Yess but only a stalking-horse or bait? It would be best to wait a while to make sure. Besides, this might be his last chance to talk with a deity.

"What is it you want?" Yess said. He bit off a small piece of the candle and began chewing.

"Can you give it to me?" Carmody said. "Not that I really care. I'm accustomed to taking what I want. Charity—in giving or in receiving—is not one of my vices."

"That'd be one of the few vices you don't have," Yess said. He looked calmly at the Earthman, then smiled. "What do you want?"

"That reminds me of the story of the fairy prince," Carmody replied. "I want you."

Yess raised his feathery eyebrows. "Not really. It is obvious you're a disciple of Algul. It shines out from every pore of your skin, it radiates with every beat of your heart. There is evil on your breath."

Staring, Yess cocked his head. Then he closed his eyes.

"But yet . . . there's something."

He opened his eyes. "You poor devil. You miserable suffering conceited cockroach. You're dying at the same time you boast you're living as no other man dares to live. You . . ."

"Shut up!" Carmody shouted. Then he smiled and softly said, "You're very good at needling, aren't you? But you'd never have stung me if it weren't for what I've gone through, for the hellish effects of this Night. Enough to drive many men mad."

He pointed his gun at Yess. "You'll not get a rise out of me again. But you can congratulate yourself on having done what few have—although those few aren't alive to brag about it."

He gestured with the gun at the candlestick in Yess' hand.

"Why in the name of insanity are you eating that? Churchmice may be poor. But gods that live in temples are poor also?"

"You have never eaten such rich food," Yess replied. "This is the most expensive candle in the world. It is made from the ground-up bones of my predecessor, a flour mixed with the wax excreted by the divine trogur bird. The trogur is sacred to my Mother, as you may know. There are only twenty-one of these most beautiful of all birds living on my planet, or anywhere in the universe, and they are tended by the priestesses of the temple of the Isle of Vantrebo.

"Every seven years, just before the Night begins, a little

pinch of bone dust from the Yess who died 763 years ago is worked into the trogur wax. The candle fashioned from the god's dust and the wax is set on this table, and the taper is lit. I sit here and wait while the billionfold Sleepers turn and toss and groan in their drugged Sleep. And while the nightmares howl and rave and kill on the streets of Kareen.

"When the candle has burned a little, I snuff out the flame. And, in accordance with the eons-old ritual, I eat the candle. By doing so, I commune with the dead god—who is at the same time living—and I partake of his divinity. I refresh myself with his godhood.

"Some time, perhaps this Night, I shall die. And my flesh will be stripped from my bones. My bones will be ground into a flour, and the flour will be mixed with trogur wax and made into a candle. Septennial by septennial, a part of me will be burned as an offering to my people and my Mother. The smoke from the burning candle will arise and drift through the ventilating system and go out into the air of the Night. And I will not only be burned, I will be eaten by the god who follows me. That is, if the god is Yess.

"For an Algul does not eat a Yess, nor a Yess eat an Algul. Evil hungers for evil, and good for good."

Carmody grinned and said, "You really believe all that nonsense?"

"I know."

"It's all primitive magic," Carmody said. "And you, a so-called civilized being, are hoodwinking your disciples, the poor, blind, superstition-staggered fools."

"Not so. If I were on Earth, your accusation might be justified. But you've gotten this far through the Night—an ill omen for me—and you must know by now that anything is possible."

"I'm sure it's all explainable by physical means as yet unknown. I just don't care. I'll tell you one thing. You're going to die."

Yess smiled and said, "Who isn't?"

"I mean right now!" Carmody snarled.

"I'ved lived 763 years. I'm getting tired, and a tired god is not good for the people. Nor does my Mother wish a feeble son. So, whether Yess or Algul triumph tonight, I must die.

"I'm ready. If you were not the instrument of my death, another would be."

Carmody shouted, "I'm no one's tool! I do what I want,

56

and any plans I carry out are mine! Mine alone, do you hear!"

Yess smiled again. "I hear. Are you trying to drive yourself into a rage which will be strong enough to allow you to kill me?"

Carmody squeezed the trigger. Yess and the chair on which he sat slid backward from the impact of the stream of exploding bullets. Flesh and blood rose in little spurts, collected into tiny balls, drifted around him, and fell down in a shower on him. His head flew apart. His arms rose upward and over, and his legs kicked up. The motion carried him over backward, and he fell with a crash.

Carmody quit firing only when the clip was empty. Then he bent down and placed the light on the floor. By its illumination, he ejected the clip and replaced it with a fresh one.

His heart was beating savagely; his hands shook. This was the culmination of his career, his masterpiece. He liked to think of himself as an artist, a great artist in crime, if not the greatest. Sometimes he would laugh at the idea and sneer at himself. But he thought of it too often, therefore he must truly believe in it. If there were artists, he was one. No one could surpass him now. Who else had murdered a god?

It was, however, a little sad. What could he do now to top this?

He would think of something. In a universe this large, something even more superb waited for him. All he had to do was get out of this situation and look for another even more challenging.

For one thing, he could not count this as a complete success unless he got out alive and uncaptured. A true work of art had to be finished to the last and least detail. He would not be caught. He was no moth to burn himself in the flame for the beauty of the act.

Carmody took from his beltbag a small flat case. After uncapping it, he squeezed it, and its liquid contents squirted out over the body. Satisfied that the corpse was covered with a film of the fluid, he retreated from it. Another case, much smaller than the first, came out of his bag. He threw his cloak up to shield his face, aimed the case, and squeezed. The spray from a tiny nozzle at its end struck the film of liquid. Yess burst into flames. Smoke and the stench of burning flesh rose upward, then spread out.

Carmody smiled. The Kareenans would not be able to

make a holy candle from the bone flour of their god. The panpyric would not stop oxidizing until the entire body was ashes.

But there was the half-eaten candle dropped by Yess when the bullets struck him. Carmody stooped and picked it up. At first, he intended to burn it, too. Then he grinned. And he ate the candle. The waxy stuff had a faintly bitter taste, not objectionable. He downed it easily, smiling at the thought that his eating of the candle was a unique event, whereas the assassination was only of historical importance. Previous Yesses had been killed, although not by an Earthman. But never, as far as he knew, had anyone but the godson of Boonta eaten the god-candle.

While he ate, he looked for exits by the glare of the fire, through the shifting windows afforded by the curls of smoke. He saw, behind the legs of Boonta, a hole in the wall. Somehow, he had missed it before when he had passed his flashlight beam over the wall. It was no higher than his head and very narrow. In fact, on walking to it he found that he would have to turn sideways if he were to get through it.

Now, he paid for past self-indulgence. His belly was too big; it caused him to jam in the hole like a slightly oversize cork in the neck of a wine bottle.

Even as he struggled and cursed, he wondered how others got through this hole. Then it came to him that many men just would not be able to use it. Therefore, this was not the usual door to whatever lay behond. What kind of a door, then, was it?

A trap!

He tore himself loose and ran a few steps away. When he turned, he saw that the archway, which had seemed to be of stone, like the wall in which it was set, was slowly closing.

So, part of the wall, at least, was composed of pseudosilicon. But the knowledge would do him no good. He did not have whatever key was needed to open a way for him.

Voices rose behind him. Men and women shouted. He whirled to see the door through which he had entered, and which had shut behind him, now gaping wide. A number of Kareenans had already passed through it. Behind them were others. Those in front were pointing with horror at the burning corpse.

John Carmody shouted and dashed toward them through the smoke. Some tried to stop him, but he shot them down. Those in the doorway either jumped through and hurled themselves out of his path or ran back out into the purple haze.

Carmody ran after them. He was coughing, and his eyes were burning and tearful. But he kept on running until he had gone through the outer door and his lungs were rid of the smoke and the stink. Then he slowed down to a fast walk. A quarter of a kilometer away, he stopped. Something was lying on the avenue before him. It resembled a man, but it was stiff and hard, and there was a quality about it and the rigidity of limbs that made him investigate it.

It was the life-sized statue of Ban Dremon, tumbled from its pedestal.

He looked up at the pedestal. Ban Dremon—another one— stood there in what should have been an empty place.

He gripped the edge of the marble base, which was a foot above his head, and with one easy powerful graceful motion pulled himself up and then over. The next moment, gun in hand, he was eye to eye with the statue.

No statue. A man, a native.

He was in the same attitude as the dislodged Ban Dremon, the right arm held out in salute, the left holding a baton, the mouth open as if to give a command.

Carmody touched the skin of the face, so much darker than the normal Kareenan's, yet not so dark as the bronze of the statue.

It was hard, smooth and cold. If it was not metal, it would pass for it. As near as he could determine in the uncertain light, the eyeballs had lost their light color. He pressed his thumbs in on them and found that they resisted like bronze. But when he stuck his finger from his left hand in the open mouth, he felt the back part of the tongue give a little, as if the flesh beneath the metallic covering were still soft. The mouth, however, was dry as any statue's.

Now how, he thought, could a man turn his protoplasm, which had only a very minute trace of copper and, as far as he remembered, no tin, into a solid alloy? Even if those elements were present in large enough quantities to form bronze, what of the heat needed?

The only explanation he could think of was that the sun was furnishing the energy and the human body was furnishing the blueprints and, somehow, the machinery necessary. The psyche had free scope during the seven nights of the Chance; it utilized, however unconsciously, forces that must exist at all times around it but of which it had no knowledge.

If that were so, he thought, then man must be, potentially,

a god. Or if god was a term too strong, then he must be a titan. A rather stupid titan, however, blind, a Cyclops with a cataract.

Why couldn't a man have this power at other times than the Night? This vast power to bend the universe to *his* will? Nothing would be impossible, nothing. A man could move from one planet to the next without a spaceship, could step from the Avenue of the Temple of Boonta on Dante's Joy some 1,500,000 light-years to Broadway in Manhattan on Earth. Could become anything, do anything, perhaps hurl suns through space as easily as a boy hurled a baseball. Space and time and matter would no longer be walls, would be doorways to step through.

A man could become anything. He could become a tree, like Mrs. Kri's husband. Or, like this man, a statue of bronze, somehow digging with invisible hands into the deep earth, abstracting minerals, fusing them without the aid of furnace walls and heat, with no knowledge of chemical composition, and depositing them directly in his cells without immediately killing himself.

There was one drawback. Eventually, having gotten what he wanted, he would die. Though able to bring about the miracle of metamorphosis, he could not bring about the miracle of living on.

This half-statue would die, just as Skelder would die when his insane lust swelled that monstrous member which he had grown to complete his lust, swelled it until it became larger than he and he, now its appendage, would find himself immobile, unable to do anything but feed himself and it and wear his heart out trying to pump enough blood to keep himself, and it, the parasite grown larger than the host, alive. He would die, just as Ralloux would die in the heat of an imagined flame of hell. They would all die unless they reversed the leap of mind and flow of flesh that hurtled them into such rich sea-changes.

And what, he thought, what about you, John Carmody? Is Mary what you want? Why should you? And what harm can her resurrection do to you? The others are obviously suffering, doomed, but you can see no doom to you in yourself giving birth to Mary again, no suffering. Why are you an exception?

I am John Carmody, he whispered. *Always have been, am, will be an exception.*

From behind and below him came a loud roar like a lion's. Men shouted. Another roar. A snarling. A man screamed as if in a death agony. Another roar. Then a strange sound as if a great bag had burst. Vaguely, Carmody felt that his ankles were wet.

He looked around in surprise and saw that the moon had gone down and the sun had risen. What had he been doing all night? Standing here on this pedestal dreaming away the purple hours?

He blinked and shook his head. He had allowed himself to be caught up in the bronze thoughts of this statue, had felt as it did, had slowed time and let it lap around him gently and dreamily, just as he had experienced the hard scarlet lust of Skelder, Mary's meltingness and liquid movements toward the satyr-priest, the impact of bullets tearing into her, her terror of death, of dissolvingness, and Ralloux' agony of flesh in his sheet of flame and agony of soul over man's damnation—just as he had felt all these, so now he had fallen prey to this creature's mineral philosophy; and might perhaps have ended as it had, if something had not jarred him out of the fatal contemplation. Even now, coming out of his—coma?—he felt the temptation of the silent peace, of letting time and space flow by, sweetly and softly.

But in the next second he came fully awake. He had tried to move away and found that he was anchored more than mentally. The finger he'd put into the statue's mouth was clamped tight between its teeth. No matter how violently he pulled away, he could not get it loose. There was no pain at all, only a numbness. This, he supposed, was because the circulation was cut off. Still, there should be some pain. If this sharing of thoughts had gone so far that his own flesh had changed . . .

The man-statue must not have been completely transformed; there must have been feeling left in the soft back part of the tongue. Reacting automatically—or maybe maliciously—it had slowly closed its jaws during the night, and when the sun saw the process of casting flesh into bronze complete, its jaws were almost shut. Now they would never open, for the soul within it was gone. Or, at least, Carmody could detect no thoughts or feeling emanating from it.

He looked around him, anxious not only because he did not know yet how to get free of this trap but because of his exposed position. What made things worse was that he'd dropped the gun. It lay at his feet, but, though he bent his knees and reached down for it with his left hand, his fingertips were several inches away.

Straightening up, he allowed himself the luxury of a firecracker-string of curses. It was ridiculous, this verbal explosion, of no practical use whatever. But he certainly felt a little less tense.

He looked up and down the street. Nobody in sight.

He looked down, remembering then that he had had the impression his legs had been wetted during the night. Dried blood caked his sandals and stained the green and white stripes of his fashionably painted legs.

He muttered, "Oh, no, not again," thinking of the shower of blood in Mrs. Kri's kitchen. But a further examination showed him that Mary was not responsible. The stuff had spurted from wounds made in the body of a monster, which lay face up at the base of the pedestal, its dead eyes staring at the purplish sky. It was twice as tall as the average Kareenan and was covered with a bluish feathery hair. Apparently its body hairs, once no thicker than those of an Earthman, had sprouted into a dense mat. Its legs and feet had broadened, like an elephant's, to support its weight. From the hips, grew a long thick tapering tail that would in time have rsembled that of a Tyrannosaurus rex. The hands had degenerated into talons, and the face had assumed a bestial angle, slanting out, the jawbones thickening, powered with great muscles, equipped with sharp teeth. These were fastened down on an arm that it had torn from some unlucky man, probably one of those who had killed it during the fight that must have taken place. But of the others there was no sign except great stains on the street and sidewalk.

Then six men walked around the corner and halted staring at him. Though they seemed unarmed, there was something in the concentration of their expressions that alarmed him. Violently he jerked upon his finger, again and again until, panting, sweating, he could only look into the rigid grin and fixed eyes of the statue and swear at it. Once, he thought, this thing was human and therefore could have been dealt with, being of weak flesh and blood. But now, dead and of unyielding, *uncaring* metal, it was past argument, past cunning words.

He ground his teeth in silent agony, and he thought, *If they won't help me, and there's no reason why they should, then I must sacrifice my finger. That's logical; that is if I want to get free again. It is possible to get my knife from my pocket and . . .*

One of the men said, mockingly, and as if he had been reading Carmody's thoughts, "Go ahead, Earthman, cut it off! That is, if you can possibly endure to mutilate your precious flesh!"

For the first time, Carmody recognized the man as Tand.

He had no chance to reply, for the others began to jeer, making fun of his having been caught in such a ridiculous way, asking him if he always made a public spectacle of himself like this. They hooted and laughed and slapped their thighs and each other's backs in typically uninhibited Kareenan fashion.

"This is the pipsqueak who thought he would kill a god!" howled Tand. "Behold the great deicide, caught like any baby with his finger in the jam jar!"

Keep cool, Carmody, they can't touch you.

That was a fine thing to say, and it meant exactly nothing. He was tired, tired, his proud bristling-forward bearing gone with the strength that seemed to have drained from his body. If his finger did not hurt because it was of frozen metal, his feet certainly made up for it. They felt as if he'd been standing on them for days.

Suddenly, he felt panic. How long had he been upon this pedestal? How much time had flowed by? How much time did he have left before the Night of Light was over?

"Tand," said one of the men, "do you honestly think that this would-be statue might have the Power?"

"Look at what he has done so far," replied Tand. He spoke to Carmody. "You have slain the old Yess, friend. He knew that it was to happen, and he told me so before the Night began.

"Now, we six are looking for one more to make the Seven Lovers of the Great Mother, the Seven Fathers of the baby Yess."

"So you lied to me!" snarled Carmody. "You weren't going to Sleep, then?"

"If you will recall my exact words," said Tand, "you will see that I did not lie. I told you the truth but ambiguously. You chose the particular interpretation."

"Friends," spoke another man, "I think we are wasting our time here and giving the Enemy an advantage we may not be able to overcome. This man, despite his tremendous power, which I can sense in him even without probing—this man, I say, is one of the dirty-souled. In fact, I doubt if he does have a soul. Or, if he does, it is a fragment, a rag, a minuscule, a tiny little thing cowering in the deep and the darkness, afraid to have anything to do with the body, allowing the body to operate as it will, refusing to take any responsibility, refusing to admit even its own existence."

The others seemed to find this very funny, for they laughed uproariously and added remarks of their own.

Carmody trembled. Their amused contempt struck him like six hammers, one after the other, then all at once, then one after the other, like an anvil chorus. It was intensified many times because he shared in it at the same time that he felt its impact, as if he were both transmitter and receiver. He who had always thought he was *above* being affected by anyone's contempt or laughter had suddenly found that it was not altitude that protected him but a barrier built up *around* him. And the defense had crumbled.

Wearily, hopelessly, he began jerking on the finger, then, as he saw six other strangers walking down the street toward him, he gave up. These men were also unarmed and walked with the same proud bearing possessed by the other group. They, too, stopped before him but ignored the first-comers.

"Is this the man?" said one.

"I think he is," replied another.

"Should we release him?"

"No. If he wishes to be one of us, he will release himself."

"But if he wishes to be one of *them* he will also release himself."

"Earthman," said a third, "you are being honored above all others—indeed you are the first man not born on this planet ever to be so honored."

"Come," said a fourth, "let us go to the Temple and there lie with Boonta and so father Algul, the true prince of this world."

Carmody began to feel less humiliated. Apparently, he was important, not only to the second group, but to the first. Though if the first wanted him for something, they had a strange way of enlisting him.

What made the procedure so peculiar was that no man in the two groups was distinguished by any conventional marks of good or evil. All were handsome, vigorous, and seemingly self-confident. The only difference in their bearing was that the first, those who spoke for Yess, seemed to be having a good time, and were not afraid to lose their dignity in laughter. The second were uniformly grave and somewhat stiff.

They must need me badly, he thought.

"What will you give me?" he said very loudly, encompassing both groups in one glance.

The men of the first group looked at each other, shrugged

their shoulders, and Tand said, "We will give you nothing you can't give yourself."

The spokesman for the newcomers, a tall young man, almost too handsome, said, "When we go into the Temple and there lie with Boonta as the Dark Mother, and father Algul her Dark Son, you will experience an ecstasy that cannot be described because you have never felt anything like it before. And during the years that it will take the babe to grow into manhood and godhood, you will be one of his regents, and there will be nothing in this world denied you—"

"Even," broke in Tand, "the fear of these others killing you so they may not have to share any of the riches which they cannot possibly spend during their lifetime. For it is true that when the seven evil Fathers triumph, they always plot against each other after Algul is born. They are forced to, because they cannot trust each other. And it has always happened that only one survives, and when Algul comes to manhood, he kills that one, because he cannot endure having a mortal Father."

"What is to prevent Algul from being killed by one of his Fathers?" asked Carmody.

Even in the violet light, he could see the men of the second group turn pale. They looked at each other. "Though he is a baby who must be fed and have his diapers changed, Algul is yet a god," said Tand. "That is, being a god, he is the sum and essence of the spirit of those who created him. And, as most men wish for immortality, he, representing them, is immortal. That is, he would live forever if his creators did, too. But, being evil, he cannot trust his fathers, and so they must die. And when they do, he begins to age and eventually dies. Though potentially immortal, he is dead the day he is born because the seeds of evil are in him, and the seeds flower into distrust and hate."

"This is all very fine," said Carmody. "Why, then, does Yess, the supposedly good god, also age and die?"

The men of Algul laughed, and their leader said, "Well spoken, Earthman."

Patiently, as if talking to a child, Tand replied, "Yess, though a god, is also a man, a being of flesh and blood. As such he is limited, and he works within the bounds set for flesh and blood. Like all men, he must die. Furthermore, he is the sum and essence of the predominating spirit of the people who lived at the time he was born—or created, whichever term you prefer. Those who Sleep have as much to do with the formation and tempering of his body and spirit as

65

we seven Wakers do. The Sleepers dream, and the collective force of their dreaming decides which god shall be born during the Night, and also what his spirit—or what you call his personality—shall be. If the inclination of the people who Sleep has been toward evil during the years preceding the Night, then it is likely that Algul will be born. If toward good, then it is likely that Yess will be born. We would-be Fathers are not actually the determining factors. We are the agents, and the Sleepers, the two billion people of our world, are the will."

Tand paused, stared hard at Carmody as if trying to impress his sincerity upon him, and said, "I will be frank. You are so important partly because you *are* an Earthman; a man from another star. Only lately have we Kareenans become very much aware of alien religions, of what their existence implies. We have become aware that the Great Mother, or God, or the Prime Cause, or whatever you wish to term the Creator of the universe, is not restricted in Her interest to our little cloud of dust, that She has scattered Her creatures everywhere.

"Therefore, the Sleepers, knowing that man is not alone, that he has blood-brothers everywhere that life may be, outward to infinity and to eternity, wish to have as a Father one of these strangers from the stars. Yess, reborn, will not be the old Yess. He will be as different from the old man who died, his predecessor, as any baby is from his father. He will be, we hope, part alien, because of his alien heritage. And during his princehood over us, he will enable us to understand and become one with these strangers from the stars, and we will be better men because of him and his heritage. That is one reason, Carmody, why we desire you."

Tand pointed at his Enemies.

"And these six want you also as seventh, but not for quite the same reason. If you are one of the Fathers of Algul, then perhaps Algul may extend his dominion past this planet and to the stars. And they, through Algul, will share in this cosmic loot."

Carmody felt hope—and craving—surge within him, bringing him strength from somewhere in his exhausted flesh. To take for yourself the richest planets, as you would the biggest diamonds for a necklace! String them on a cord of space and wear them around your neck! With the vast powers he would undoubtedly have as Algul's regent, he could do anything! Nothing barred!

It was then that the second group must have decided that

66

the right moment had come, for they suddenly launched at him the collective force of their feelings. And he, being wide open, reeled beneath them.

Dark, dark, dark . . .

Ecstasy . . .

He, John Carmody, would be forever John Carmody as he now knew him, inviolate, strong, defiant, bending or destroying anything in the way of what he wanted. No danger here of his changing, of becoming something other than what he now was. Body, mind, and soul, he would in the flame of this dark ecstasy become hard as a diamond, resisting all change, permanent, forever John Carmody. The race of man might die around him, suns grow cold, planets slow and fall into their parent suns, but he, John Carmody, would travel outwards with the expanding universe, landing upon freshly born planets, living there until they grew old and died, then setting out again. And always and forever himself, today and tomorrow, unchanging, the same hard-and-bright-as-a-diamond John Carmody.

Then the first group opened themselves up. But instead of launching at him their concentrated essence, like a spear, they merely lowered the wall and allowed him to attack or do whatever he wished. There was not the slightest hint of assault or force, nor the feeling the fathers of Algul gave of withholding something deep within themselves in reserve. They were wide open and transparent to the depths of their beings.

John Carmody could no more resist attacking than a hungry tiger who sees a goat tethered to a tree.

Light, light, light . . .

Ecstasy . . .

But not the hardening, setting-for-ever ecstasy of the others. This was threatening, frightening, for it exploded him, dissolved, sent him flying in a thousand bits outwards.

Screaming silently, in mental anguish, he tried to collect the hundred thousand fragments, to bring them back, fused again into the image of the old John Carmody. The pain of destroying himself was unendurable.

Pain? It was the same as the ecstasy. How could pain and ecstasy be the same thing?

He didn't know. All he did know was that he had recoiled from the six of Yess. Their lack of walls was their defense. Not for anything would he again attack them. Destroy John Carmody?

"Yes," said Tand, though Carmody had not spoken. "You

must die first; you must dissolve that image of the old John Carmody, and build a new image, a better one, just as the newly born Yess will be better than the old god who died."

Abruptly, Carmody turned from both groups and, reaching in his pocket, drew out the switchknife. His thumb pressed the button in the handle and the blade shot out like a blue-gray tongue, like the tongue of the snake that had bitten him.

There was but one way to get loose from the bronze jaws. He did it.

It hurt, but not so badly as he thought it would. Nor did he bleed as much as he had expected. He mentally ordered the blood vessels to close. And they, like flowers at the approach of night, obeyed.

But the work of sawing through flesh and bone left him panting as if he'd run several kilometers. His legs trembled, and the faces below him blurred, and ran into two broad white featureless faces. He couldn't last long.

The leader of the men of Algul stepped forward and held out his arms. "Jump, Carmody," he called joyfully. "Jump! I will catch you; my arms are strong. Then we will scatter this weak, sniveling brood, and go to the temple and there—"

"Wait!"

The woman's voice, coming from behind them, loud and commanding, yet at the same time musical, froze them.

He looked up, over the heads of the men.

Mary.

Mary, alive and whole again, as he had seen her before he emptied his gun into her face. Unchanged, except for one thing. Her belly was swollen enormously; it had grown since he had last seen her and was now ripe to give birth to the life within her.

The leader of the men of Algul said to Carmody, "Who is this Earthwoman?"

Carmody, standing on the edge of the base, ready to leap down, hesitated and opened his mouth to reply. But Tand spoke first.

"She is his wife. He killed her upon Earth and fled here. But he created her the first night of the Sleep."

"Ahhhh!"

The seven of Algul sucked in their breath and drew back.

Carmody blinked at them. Apparently, Tand's information held implications he didn't see.

"John," she said, "it is no use your murdering me again and again. I always rise. I always will. And I am ready to

68

bear the child you did not want; he will be here within the hour. At dawn."

Quietly, but with a tremor in his voice that betrayed the great strain he felt, Tand said, "Well, Carmody, which shall it be?"

"Which?" said Carmody, sounding stupid even to himself.

"Yes," said the leader of Algul, stepping back beneath the pedestal. "Which shall it be? Shall the baby be Yess or Algul?"

"So that is it!" said Carmody. "The economy of the Goddess, of Nature, of What-have-you. Why create a baby when one is at hand?"

"Yes," said Mary loudly, her voice still musical but demanding, like a bronze bell. "John, you do not want our baby to be as you were, do you? A frozen dark soul? You do want him to be of heat and light, don't you?"

"Man," said Tand, "don't you see that you have already chosen who the babe shall be? Don't you know that she has no brain of her own, that what she says is what you think, really think and truly desire in the depths of your soul? Don't you know that you are putting her words into her mouth, that her lips move as you direct them?"

Carmody almost fainted, but not from weakness and hunger of body.

Light, light, light . . . Fire, fire, fire . . . Let himself dissolve. Like the phoenix, he would rise again. . . .

"Catch me, Tand," he whispered.

"Jump," said Tand, laughing loudly. A roar of laughter and of cries that sounded like hallelujahs burst from the men of Yess.

But the men of Algul shouted in alarm and began running away in all directions.

At the same time the dark purplish haze began to grow lighter, to turn pale violet. Then, suddenly, the ball of fire was above the horizon, and the violet light was white again, as if someone had yanked aside a veil.

And those of the men of Algul who were still in sight staggered, fell to the ground, and died in the midst of convulsions that threw them from side to side and that broke their bones. For a time they thrashed like chickens with their heads cut off, then, bloody-mouthed, lay still.

"Had you chosen otherwise," said Tand, still embracing Carmody after his leap downward, "we would be lying in the dust of the street."

They began walking toward the temple, forming a circle

around Mary, who walked slowly and stopped now and then as the pains struck her. Carmody, walking behind her, gritted his teeth and moaned softly, for he too felt the pangs. He was not alone; the others were biting their lips and holding their hands tight upon their bellies.

"And what happens afterward to her—to it?" he whispered to Tand. He whispered because, even if he knew that this Mary-thing was not self-conscious, was really manipulated by his thoughts—and now by those of the others, too—he had become suddenly sensitive to the feelings of other people. He did not want to take a chance on hurting her, even if such a thing did not seem possible.

"Her work will be done when Yess is born," said the Kareenan. "She will die. She is dying now, began dying when the Sleep ended. She is being kept alive by our combined energies and by the unconscious will of the infant within her. Let us hurry. Soon the Wakers will be coming from their vaults, not knowing if this time Yess or Algul won, not knowing if they must rejoice or weep. We must not leave them long in doubt, but must get to the Temple. There we will enter the holy chamber of the Great Mother, will lie in mystical love and procreation with Her, in that act that cannot be described but can only be experienced. The swollen body of this creation of your hate and your love will deliver the baby and will die. And then we must wash and wrap the baby and have him ready to show the adoring people."

He squeezed Carmody's hand affectionately, then tightened his grip as the pangs struck again. But Carmody did not feel the bone-squeezing strength because he was fighting his own pain, hot and hard in his own belly, rising and falling in waves, the terrible hurt and awful ecstasy of giving birth to divinity.

That pain was also the light and fire of himself still exploding and dissolving into a million pieces. But now there was no panic, only a joy he had never known in accepting this light and fire and in the sureness that he would at the end of this destruction be whole, be one as few men are.

Through this pain, this joy, this sureness was a lacing of determination that he would pay for what he had done. Not pay in the sense that he would forever be plunged into self-punishment, into gloom and remorse and self-hate. No, that was a sickness, that was not the healthy way to pay. He must make up for what he had been and had done. This universe, though it still ran like a hard cold machine and presented no really sweet-smiling face to mankind, this world could be changed.

What means he would employ and just what sort of goal he would choose, he did not know now. That would come later. At this moment, he was too busy carrying out the final act of the drama of the Sleep and the Awakening.

Suddenly he saw the faces of two men he had never expected to see any more. Ralloux and Skelder. The same, yet transfigured. Gone was the agony on Ralloux's face, replaced by serenity. Gone was the harshness and rigidity on Skelder's face, replaced by the softness of a smile.

"So you two came through all right," Carmody said throatily.

Wonderingly, he noted that one was still clad in his monk's robes but that the other had cast them off and was dressed in native clothes. He would have liked to find out just why this man accepted and the other rejected, but he was sure that both had their good and sufficient reasons, otherwise they would not have survived. The same look was on both their faces, and at the moment it did not matter which path either had chosen for his future.

"So you both came through," Carmody murmured, still scarcely able to believe it.

"Yes," replied one of them, which one Carmody couldn't determine, so dreamlike did everything seem, except for the reality of the waves of pain within his bowels. "Yes, we both came through the fire. But we were almost destroyed. On Dante's Joy, you know, you get what you really want."

PART TWO

"And now I must go back to Kareen?" Father John Carmody said. "After twenty-seven years!"

He had been sitting quietly enough while Cardinal Faskins told him what the Church wanted of him. But he could be motionless no longer. Although he did not soar from his chair, he rose swiftly, arms up and then out, as if he intended to fly. And that posture expressed what he wished to do at that moment—wing away from the cardinal and all he represented.

He began pacing back and forth across the polished, close-grained, dark gooma-wood floors, his hands clasped behind him for a while, then unlocked, only to rejoin above his stomach. Outwardly, he had not changed much; he was still a little porcupine of a man. But now he wore the maroon garb of a priest of the Order of St. Jairus.

Cardinal Faskins stooped in his chair, his green eyes bright above the big hooked nose. His head turned this way and then that to keep the pacing Carmody in view. He looked like an aged hawk uncertain of his prey but determined to make a move at the first chance. His face was wrinkled; his hair, white. A half-decade ago, he had voluntarily given up jerries, and his one hundred and twenty-seven years were catching up with him.

Suddenly John Carmody stopped before the cardinal. He frowned and said, "You really think I'm the only one qualified for this mission?"

"Best qualified," Faskins said. He straightened a little and placed his hands on the arms of the chair as if to shove himself upward and out on the strike.

"I've told you once why this is so urgent. Once should be enough; you're an intelligent man. You're also dedicated to the Church. Otherwise, you would not have been considered for the episcopal seat."

The reproach, although unvoiced, was detected and briefly considered by the priest. Carmody knew that his decision to marry again, almost immediately after the Church had relaxed its discipline of celibacy, had disappointed the cardinal. Faskins had worked hard to make sure that Carmody would become the bishop of the diocese of the colonial planet of Wildenwooly. He had fought a political battle with those who believed that Carmody was too unorthodox in his methods of carrying out Christian policies. None questioned the orthodoxy of his belief; it was the offhand, or freehand, way he acted that was in doubt. Was it suitable that such an "eccentric"—one of the kinder words used—should wear the mitre of a bishop?

Then, when Carmody had seemed to be in, he had married and thus removed himself from consideration. And the accusations of his enemies seemed to be vindicated. But the cardinal had never directly reproached Carmody.

Now, John Carmody wondered if the cardinal was not using this "betrayal" as a lever? Or did he himself just feel so guilty about it that he was projecting?

Faskins glanced at the pale yellow letters flashing on the screen at the end of the great room. "You have two hours to get ready," he said. "You'll have to start now if you're going to get to the port on time."

He became silent, his gaze remaining on the clock.

Carmody laughed softly and said, "What can I do? I'm not being ordered, just told I must volunteer. Very well. I'll do it. You knew I would. And I'll get started packing. But I have to tell Anna. It's going to be a hell of a shock to her!"

Faskins shifted uneasily. "The life of a priest isn't always an easy one. She knew that."

"I know she knows it!" Carmody said fiercely. "She told me what you said to her after I asked for permission to marry. You painted a black picture indeed!"

"I'm sorry, John," Faskins replied with a slight smile. "Reality is sometimes not golden."

"Yes. And you're noted for your reticence—"Few Phrases" Faskins, they call you—but you talked up a tornado with her."

"Again, I'm sorry."

"Forget it," Carmody said. "It's done. I'm not the least bit sorry about Anna. My only regret is that I couldn't have married her years ago. I baptized her, you know, and she's lived all her life in my parish."

He hesitated, then went on, "She's pregnant, too. That's another reason why I hate to give her this shock."

The cardinal said nothing. Carmody muttered, "Excuse me. I'll only be about ten minutes packing. I'll phone Anna and get her home. She can ride to the port with us."

The cardinal, unable to repress his alarm, stood up.

"I don't think I should be with you, John. You two should be alone for a while, and the only time you'll have will be on the ride to the port."

"Nothing doing," the priest said. "You're going to suffer along with me. Anyway, I don't intend to be alone. Anna can go with me as far as Springboard. There'll be a long wait there, and we can be alone. You're coming down with us!"

The cardinal shrugged. Carmody poured another Scotch for him and went to the bedroom. He unfolded a suitcase and threw it on the bed. One small case would be enough for him. Anna, even though her trip would be short, would probably insist on taking two large ones for herself. She liked to be ready for any sartorial emergency. After unfolding two cases for her, he pressed a tiny button on the flat disc

73

strapped to his right wrist. Its center glowed; a pinging rose thinly to his ears.

He continued to pack, not wishing to waste any time and knowing that she would soon respond to his call. But when all his clothes were packed, and he noted that ten minutes had passed, he began to worry. He activated the large phone on the table by the bed and spoke Mrs. Rougon's code number. She answered at once. On seeing him, her plump face brightened. "Father John! I was just about to call you! I mean, Anna! She was supposed to be through with her shopping and here a half-hour ago. I thought maybe she forgot and came home instead."

"She's not here."

"Maybe she took her caller off for some reason and forgot to put it back on. You know how she is, a little absentminded sometimes, especially since she's been thinking about the baby. Oh, good heavens, Alice is crying! I have to go now! But do call back when you find Anna! Or I'll tell her to call you as soon as she gets here!"

Carmody at once phoned Rheinkord's Fashion Shop. The clerk told him that Mrs. Carmody had left about fifteen minutes ago.

"Did she by any chance say where she was going?"

"Yes, Father. She did mention she was going to the hospital for a minute. She wanted to give some comfort to Mr. Augusta; she said he hasn't been doing very well since his accident."

Carmody sighed relief and said, "Thank you very much."

He called the Way Station of St. Jairus and got immediate attention. The monitor looked a little awed at seeing the founder of the hospital himself.

"Mrs. Carmody left five minutes ago, Father. No, she didn't say where she was going."

Carmody called Mrs. Rougon back. "You'll have to forego your chat, I'm afraid. Tell my wife she's to call me immediately; it's very important."

He disconnected but still was not satisfied. Why could he not get her on the caller? A malfunction in the instrument? Possible but not very likely. A caller did not wear out and had no discrete parts to go wrong. It could be put out of commission only by something like a sledgehammer blow. But it could be left off. Perhaps Mrs. Rougon was right. Anna could have removed it before washing her hands, although soap and water or even sonics would not harm the device. Then she could have forgotten to replace it.

74

There was the possibility that a thief had taken the caller, since men stole even now in a land of plenty, always for a reason sufficient to them.

He returned to his packing. Anna would not like the helterskelter folding or his choice of her clothes, but there was no time for her to dally over her wardrobe.

The first case filled and shut, he started on the second. The phone rang. He dropped the blouse he was folding. Eagerly, he spoke the activating code and walked up to the screen even though it was not necessary. He liked to be close to anybody he talked to, even if over a phone, and especially he wanted nearness with Anna.

The face of a city policeman appeared. Carmody grunted, and his belly shrank inward as if a knife had struck it.

"Sergeant Lewis, Father," the policeman said. "I'm sorry . . . but I have bad news . . . about your wife."

Carmody did not reply. He stared at the heavy craggy face of Lewis, noting at the same time, with complete irrelevance, that a bushfly was buzzing about Lewis' head. He thought, We'll never get rid of them. All of 22nd-century science is at hand, yet bushflies and other creeping, crawling creatures multiply themselves and divide our attentions, despite all human efforts. ". . . Her tattoo was blown off, so we can't officially identify her, even if her face is recognizable, and she's been identified by some of her friends who were there," the sergeant was saying. "I'm terribly sorry, but you will have to come down and make it official."

Carmody said, "What?" and then the policeman's words sank home. Anna had left the hospital in her car. A few blocks away, a bomb under the driver's seat had gone off. Only the upper part of her body was left, and at least one arm must be gone, if the identity tattoo was destroyed.

Carmody said, "Thank you, sergeant, I'll be right down." He walked away from the phone and into the living room. The cardinal, seeing his pale face and sagging posture, jumped up from his seat, knocking his glass off the table with a crash.

Dully, Carmody told Faskins what had happened.

The cardinal wept then. Later, when Carmody came out of his shock, he knew that he had seen into the depths of Faskins' love for him, for it was said by all that Faskins had no more juice in him than an old bone. Carmody himself was dry-eyed; nothing seemed to be functioning except his arms and legs and, now and then, his mouth.

75

"I'll go with you," the cardinal said. "Only first I will call the port and cancel your passage."

"Don't do that," Carmody said. He returned to the bedroom, picked up his suitcase, and, glancing at the other suitcases, one closed and one open, walked out of the bedroom. The cardinal was staring at him.

Carmody said, "I must go."

"You're not in shape to do so."

"I know. But I will be."

The doorbell rang. Doctor Apollonios entered, bag in hand. He said, "I'm sorry, Father. Here, this will help you." He reached into his blouse pocket and brought out a pill. Carmody shook his head. "I can make it all right. Who called you?"

"I did," Faskins said. "I think you ought to take it."

"Your authority doesn't extend to medical matters," Carmody answered. A soft tocsin note pealed through the room. He put down his suitcase and went to the wall. Opening a small cover, he removed a small, thin cylinder.

"The mail," he said to no one in particular. He looked into the cubicle to see if any other mail was being recorded. The little red light was out. He closed the door and returned to his suitcase, tucking the letter into his beltbag.

On the way to the police morgue, the cardinal said, "I didn't have the heart to ask you to go on to Kareen, John. But since you yourself volunteered, I won't object. Anna . . ."

". . . Is only one human being, and the destiny of billions of others depends upon me," Carmody finished for him. "Yes, I know."

The cardinal said he would not leave this afternoon as he had planned. Despite the most pressing urgency to return to Rome, he would stay here and conduct Anna's funeral. He would make all arrangements, including the police investigation. After Carmody got to Kareen, he could expect to receive news, by letter or courier, about the results of the investigation.

"The police," Carmody said listlessly. "I wonder who could have hated me enough to kill Anna. She had no enemies. But won't the police delay me with their questions so I'll miss the ship?"

"Leave that to me," Faskins said.

Afterward, Carmody was unclear about much that happened. He lifted the sheet without any apprehension or agony and gazed for a moment at the blackened, open-mouthed face. He repeated to the police captain what he had told the cardinal. No, he had no idea who could have planted the bomb. Somebody had returned from a past Carmody had hoped would be forever obliterated and had killed Anna.

The two priests started toward the port in a taxi. They passed the headquarters of the Order of St. Jairus on Wildenwooly. Twenty-three years ago, the building had been on the outer edge of a small town. Now it was in the heart of the large capital city of the planet. Where there had been no buildings more than two stories high, dozens now reached above twenty stories. Where a man once could have walked from the center of town to its borders in twenty minutes, he would now have to walk from dawn to dusk. All the streets were paved, and most of the highways out into the farmlands were covered with griegite. When John Carmody had first come here as a lay brother of the order, he had muddied his sandals the moment he had stepped from the exit of the spaceport. And the buildings of the town had been logs and mortar. . . .

Anna. If he had not married her, he would now be sitting behind the huge shiny desk in the main office. He would be supervising the ecclesiastical affairs of his Church on a planet as large as Earth. True, Wildenwooly had a population of only fifty million, but this was fifty times what it had been when Carmody had first set foot here. It was a paradise of elbow room. Earth was jammed with people raw from rubbing against each other's skins.

Anna. If she had not married him, she would be alive today. But when he had told her that he was not sure he was doing the right thing by marrying her, she had told him she would go into a convent if she could not have him. He had laughed then and told her that she was being romantic and unrealistic. She needed a man. And if she could not have him, she would eventually find another.

There had been a furious quarrel, after which they had fallen into each other's arms. The next day, he had taken ship to Earth to make his annual report. He had spent two weeks there and left, glad to get off Earth and eager to see Anna again. The Vatican was now a cube a half-mile wide. It housed not only the Holy Father but the millions needed to run the complex government of the Church on Earth and on Earth's forty colonist planets, and the people who furnished services and goods and their families. It also contained a titanic protein-computer second in size only to the Federation's Og Boojum.

The rest of Rome was a two-mile high quadrangle around the Vatican. The Eternal Seven Hills had long ago been leveled; the Tiber ran through a plastic tube in the lower levels of Rome.

Change was the only constant in human affairs and, indeed, in the universe. Men and women were born and died ... Anna!

He cried and sobbed as if great hands within him were squeezing the breath and the tears out of him. The cardinal was rigid with embarrassment, but he pulled Carmody's head down against his chest and patted the priest's hair while he muttered jerky and awkward consolation. Presently, his body relaxed, and his own tears fell upon Carmody.

By the time they had reached the port, Carmody was sitting up and drying his eyes on a handkerchief. "I'll be all right now. For a while, anyway. I'm glad I have an excuse to get away. If I'd stayed, I might have fallen apart. What kind of an example would I be to those I've tried to support in their grief? Or to those who've listened to me preach that death is more an occasion for joy than sorrow, since glory awaits the dead and they're beyond the temptations and evils of this world? I knew damn well while I was saying all those words that they meant little. It's not until the shock and pain wear away that they're any comfort."

The cardinal did not reply. A moment later, they reached the port. This was a five-story building, covering thirty acres, and built largely of white marble quarried in the Whizaroo mountains some ninety kilometers from the capital city. Its huge main room was filled with human beings from every planet in the Federation and a number of other sentients. Most of them were here on government or other business; the minority were those who had enough money to afford first-class fares. The immigration section was in another part of the building, and there the people were not so expensively dressed nor so carefree.

The two priests walked slowly through the crowd, many of whom wore the "medusa" or "living wig," which coiled itself at regulated times to form different coiffures and also every hour passed through the entire spectrum of 100,000 colors. Many wore the half-cloaks with flaring "bartizan" shoulders and material which gave forth tinkles, the notes of which varied according to minute changes in temperature and air pressure. A few of the older people had painted

78

legs, but the rest wore boswells—tights on the surface of which appeared moving pictures of the wearer at various stages of his life, and personal statistics or capsule biographies. One expensively dressed woman had boswells which portrayed in cartoons the highlights of her life.

Carmody said goodby to His Eminence, who wanted to return to the city and start making arrangements for the funeral. He also had several letters to dictate to the officials in the Vatican, explaining why he was delayed.

The checkout required for every interstellar traveler took a half-hour. Carmody stripped off his clothes, which were taken away to be sanitized. In the physical-examination cubicle, he stood motionless for two minutes while the scanners probed intangibly into his body. At the end of that time, he was given a certificate of good health. His garments were returned with another certificate. He put back on his three-cornered, low-brimmed hat, the stiff white collar, the simple blouse, the conservatively puffed shorts, the modest codpiece, and unadorned maroon tights. From that moment until he entered the ship, he was not allowed to re-enter the other part of the building.

However, a letter, also sanitized, was delivered to him via tube. A woman's voice came through a speaker to inform him that the letter had just come off the *Mkuki,* direct from Earth. Carmody looked at the seal, which bore his name and address and that of the sender: R. Raspold. He dropped it into his beltbag with the other letter.

Meanwhile, his passport and other papers were brought up to date, checked, and validated. He had to sign a waiver whereby both the governments of Wildenwooly and the Federation were absolved of any obligation if he were to die or be injured on Kareen. He also took out insurance for the flight as far as Springboard. Half went to his order, one quarter to his daughter (begotten two years after he had become a priest), and one quarter to the governmental agency that supervised the reservations for the sentient but primitive aboriginals of Wildenwooly.

He finished a few minutes before announcement of the takeoff of his ship, the *White Mule,* a small liner of the privately owned Saxwell Stellar Line. Thus, he had a little time to study his fellow debarkees. There were four, three of whom would be getting off at planets other than Kareen. The only one whose destination was the same as his was a Raphael Abdu. He was of average height, 1.9 meters, medium stocky in build, but his hands and feet were huge. He had a broad, meaty face, a dark skin, wavy brown hair, and slight epicanthic folds that indicated some Mongolian ancestors. According to the records, he was a native of Earth and had been on Wildenwooly for several weeks. His business was listed as export-import, a term covering a multitude of interests.

A voice from the speaker asked all to sit down. A minute later, the room in which the travelers sat detached itself from the main building and moved out toward the *White Mule*. The liner was a hemisphere the flat part of which rested on the griegite-paved landing circle. Its white irradiated plastic skin gleamed in the midafternoon sun of Wildenwooly. As the mobile room approached, the seemingly unbroken surface of the *White Mule* split near the ground, and a round port swung out. The mobile, directed by remote control, nudged gently into the entrance, and its front door collapsed on itself. An officer in the green uniform of the Saxwell line entered and bade them welcome.

The passengers filed into a small chamber with only a green rug for furnishings and thence into a larger room. This was a cocktail lounge, now closed. They passed through another room, where they were handed a small document. Carmody glanced through his to see if anything new had been added, then stuck the paper into a pocket of his blouse. It contained a short history of the Saxwell line and a list of procedures for the passenger, with all of which he was familiar.

There were three levels open to passengers, first, second, and third class. Carmody had purchased a ticket for third class, in accordance with the economy required by his order. His level was a huge room that looked more like a theater than anything else, except that the screen at this moment showed the view outside the ship. The seats were arranged two abreast with aisles between the rows. Most of the eight hundred seats were filled, and the room was noisy with chatter. At that moment, Carmody wished he were in a first-class cabin, where he could have privacy. But that was out of the question, so he sat down beside a vacant seat.

A stewardess checked him to make sure he was strapped in, and asked him if he had read the rules. Would he care for a space pill? He said he did not need one.

She smiled at him and went on to the next passenger. Carmody could overhear the fellow say that he wanted another pill.

The pilot's smiling face appeared on the screen. He welcomed his passengers aboard the *White Mule*, a fine ship which had not had an accident or even been behind schedule in its ten years of service. He warned them that takeoff would be within five minutes and repeated the stewardesses' instructions not to remove the straps. After a few words about their next stop, he signed off.

The screen went blank for a second, then the 3-D projection of Jack Wenek, a well-known comedian, abruptly hovered in the air a meter in front of the screen. Carmody did not care to listen, so ignored the button which would have brought Wenek's voice to him. However, he felt that he needed something to divert himself. Or something even stronger than a diversion, something which would put his grief and problems in a different perspective. He needed immensity, awe and wonder to make him shrink.

He reached under the seat and took from the rack a helmet-shaped device with a snap-down visor. After placing it on his head, he moved the visor down over his face. Immediately, he heard the voice of an officer of the *White Mule*.

". . . Provided individually so that your fellow passengers won't have to view this if they don't wish to. Some people, encountering this for the first time, are thrown into a state of shock or hysteria."

The curved inner side of the visor leaped into solid life. Carmody could see the spaceport outside, the white, mural-decorated buildings gleaming in the bright mid-afternoon sun, the people looking out of the windows of the port buildings at the *White Mule*.

"A dozen spaceships take off every day from this port. But the spectacle, unspectacular as it is, continues to attract hundreds, even thousands, of sightseers every day on every planet of the Federation. And on every non-Federation planet, too, for sentients are just as curious as Terrestrials. Even much-traveled passengers, the port employees, and the crews of other ships do not become accustomed to this seemingly magical trick."

Carmody drummed his fingers on the arm of the chair, for he had heard similar speeches many times. At once, a voice cut in: "Are you all right, sir?"

Carmody said, "Huh?" Then he chuckled. "I'm OK. I was just a little impatient with the lecture. I've made over a hundred jumps."

"Very well, sir. Sorry to have bothered you."

He made an effort to calm himself, and settled back to watch the scene on the visor.

The first voice returned. ". . . three, two, one, zero!"

Carmody, knowing what was coming, refrained from blinking. The port was gone. The planet of Wildenwooly and the brightness of its sun were gone. Cups of burning wine hung on a black table: red, green, white, blue, violet. The one-eyed beasts of the jungle of space glared.

". . . approximately 50,000 light-years away in quote nothing flat unquote. The Earth-sized planet you were just on is too far away to be seen, and its sun is only one of the millions of stars scattered prodigally through the universe around you, 'the eternally sparked thoughts in God's mind,' to quote the great poet Gianelli.

"Just a moment. Our ship is turning now to align herself for the next jump. The protein computer which I briefly described a moment ago is comparing the angles of light from a dozen identifiable stars, each of which radiates its unique complex of spectral colors and each of which has a known spatial relation to the other. After the quote artificial brain unquote of the computer ascertains our location, it will point the ship for the next jump."

Fine horizontal and vertical lines appeared on the visor before Carmody.

"Each square of the grid is numbered for your convenience. Square 15, near the center, will contain the luminary of Wildenwooly in a few seconds. It is now in No. 16, drifting at a 45-degree angle across it. Watch it, ladies and gentlemen. It is now becoming brighter, not because it is getting closer but because we have amplified its light for your easier identification."

A yellow spark passed beneath a larger but ghostly pale blue one, then entered the corner of square fifteen. It slipped across the grid line, stopped in the middle, and bobbed up to the center.

Carmody remembered the first time he had seen this happen, so many years ago. Then he had felt a definite pain in his belly, as if his umbilical cord had been reattached, only to be savagely ripped out and to go trailing away from him through space. He had been lost, lost as never before in his life.

"The location of Wildenwooly's sun relative to the other point-stars has been determined and stored by the computer. The ship was ready several million microseconds ago to hurl itself on its next leap through the so-called subspace or nonspace. But the captain has delayed the ship because Saxwell Interstellar Lines cares about the enjoyment of its passengers. Saxwell wants its guests to see for themselves what is occurring outside the *White Mule*.

"The next jump will take us another 50,000 light-years, and we will quote emerge unquote from nonspace or extraspace, a hundred kilometers outside the extreme limits of the atmosphere of our next planetary destination, Mahomet.

"This precision is possible only because of the numerous flights that the *White Mule* has made between Wildenwooly and Mahomet. Of course, the relative positions of the two have changed since the last trip. But a cesium clock is coordinated with the computer, and the distance and angles traversed by the pertinent planets since the last trip have been calculated and compared to our present position. When the captain activates the proper control, he gives the order for the entire navigational complex of the *White Mule* to bring the calculations up to the microsecond and then to automatically jump the ship."

The officer paused, then said, "Are you ready, ladies and gentlemen? I will now count . . ."

Minimum jump, for some reason Carmody did not understand, was the length of the spacecraft. Maximum jump depended on the number of translation generators used and the power available. The *White Mule* could have passed from the Galaxy to anywhere in Andromeda in one leap. One and a half million light-years could be spanned as swiftly as the spurt of an electron down a wire. And the distance from Wildenwooly to a position just outside the atmosphere of Kareen could be spanned in four maneuvers, total "real" time sixty seconds. But the owners of the *White Mule* were more interested in making money than in displaying the powers of the vessel. Thus, there were two more planetary stops before Kareen.

The blackness and the burning globes flickered. Before Carmody was the great bow of a planet, forever taut with the pull of gravity, sunlight striking off an ocean, the darkness of a tortoise-shaped continent, the whiteness of a cloud mass like an old, huge scar on the shell of the tortoise.

Despite his previous experience, Carmody jerked back. The massy bulk was falling toward him. Then he was lost in admiration, as always, at the seeming ease and sureness of the maneuver. The complex of artificially grown cells, only three times the size of his own brain, had given the *White Mule* its true course. It had directed the jump so that the vessel popped like a rabbit out of a hat, perilously close to the upper air of Mahomet, tangent to the course of the planet around its sun and moving at the same velocity. Moreover, the *White Mule* was over the hemisphere on which it was to land.

Carmody blinked. The curve leaped at him. Another flicker of the eyelid. The visor was filled with a large lake, a mountain range, and a few clouds. The ship rocked for a few seconds, then steadied as the compensating drives took over.

A blink. The range was now a dozen mountains and the lake had expanded. On the western shore of the lake was the spiderweb outline of a city's streets and a number of huge white round spots, like a spider's eggs—the landing circles—in the center of the web.

Down on the surface, those looking upward would see the *White Mule,* if they saw it at all, only a glint of light. But in a few seconds they would hear the boom made by the *White Mule*'s first displacement of air as it had flashed from "nonspace" into the atmosphere. Then, as the ship became visible as a larger disc, another boom would follow the first. And a third.

Presently, the vessel slowed and, lightly as a balloon with a slow leak, matched its flat underside with Landing Circle Six.

Despite the two-hour layover, Carmody did not leave the ship. He did not care to go through the decontamination process on re-entering the ship; he wanted to read the two letters in his bag, and, most of all, he wished to be alone. In the cocktail lounge, he ordered a tall bourbon and then shut the door to the cubicle. After several deep swallows of his drink, he took the letters out. For several minutes, he toyed with the cylinders, his normal decisiveness missing. Which to read first, he thought, as if he had a big decision to make. Then his curiosity got the better of him, and he inserted the unidentified letter into the aperture of the 'ducer, a small box attached to the wall.

There was also a "reader" on a hook—a lightweight plastic hemisphere with a visor. He placed this over his head, lowered the visor over his eyes, and pressed the button that would run off the contents of the letter.

The interior of the visor sprang into a glow. Something appeared on it that made Carmody straighten in a reflex to get away from it. A mask was before him—a mask that looked as if it were meant to portray a face ruined by an accident.

A man's deep voice spoke. "Carmody, this letter is from Fratt. By now, your wife will be dead. You won't know why she was killed or who did it, but I will explain why.

"Many years ago you killed Fratt's son and blinded Fratt. You did it deliberately and maliciously, when it was not necessary, when you could have carried out your evil plans without harming either Fratt or Fratt's son.

"Now, if you have any humanity or sense of love in you —which is doubtful—you will know exactly how Fratt grieved, how Fratt suffered at the death of his son.

"And you will keep on suffering. Not only because of your wife, but because you will not know when or where you will die. Because you will die at Fratt's hands.

"But it will not be an easy or quick death, such as your wife was lucky enough to get. You will die slowly and in much pain, and you will pay for what you did. You will experience the same agonies as those which Fratt, your innocent victim, experienced.

"And you will know then who killed your wife and who has been thinking of nothing but your repayment for all these years.

"You will see who has never forgiven you, you foul and loathsome thing!"

The screen went blank, and the voice stopped.

Carmody raised the visor with a trembling hand and stared at the mural on the wall. He was breathing heavily. So, his guesses had been right. Some old enemy, someone he had wronged in the old and evil days had not forgotten. And for what he had done then, he had lost his wife and his greatest happiness. Anna, poor Anna . . .

He lowered the visor and ran the letter through again. Now he understood from the peculiar wording that the speaker might not be Fratt. Nor did he have a clue to the sex of Fratt. The letter had been designed to avoid this, as it had avoided any specifics of the time or place of the crime of which he was accused.

"Fratt? Fratt?" he muttered. "Fratt? The name means nothing to me. I remember no Fratt, yet I should. I have an excellent memory. But those few years were so crowded, and I was so careless of the identity of my victims. I, God forgive me, killed or even tortured many whose names I did not know.

"So it may be that I remember no Fratt because I did not

know his, or her, name. Fratt's son? That should be some clue. But I may not even have known that Fratt had a son. God!"

He took another drink and wished that it could wash away all knowledge of his past. He was not the John Carmody that Fratt had known. The name and the body might look the same but within he was not *that* John Carmody. That man was as dead as if he had truly died on Kareen.

But others had not died, and they had neither forgotten nor forgiven.

He drank another bourbon. There was nothing he could do at the moment. But, at least, he would be on his guard. Fratt would not find it easy to get at him. Nor would he find a passive victim, one weak with contrition and shame and hoping to pay for the deaths through his own, one willing to go to the sacrificial altar of his own conscience.

He struck the top of the table with his fist and almost unbalanced the glass. To hell with Fratt! If Carmody had been evil, he had shed that evil. There was more than Fratt could say for himself. If Fratt had been an innocent victim, Fratt was no longer innocent.

Then he thought, But I am responsible for turning Fratt to evil. If I had not done what I did, I would not have generated this hate in Fratt. Perhaps I twisted Fratt so much that he shed whatever good was in him, as I later shed my evil, and he became the monster that I was. Action and reaction. Turnabout is fair play. Whatever has happened or will happen, I am the guilty one.

Nevertheless, he felt the old vigor flow through his veins. Vengeance is mine, saith the Lord. But He uses all sorts of weapons with which to effect vengeance.

"No," he said to himself, and he shook his head, "I am rationalizing. I must forgive and love my enemy as a brother. That is what I have preached all these years, all these years. And I meant it. Or thought I did."

He struck the tabletop again. "But I hate! I hate! Oh, God, how I hate!"

Self-hate?

"Oh, God!" he said. "Make me see that I am wrong!"

He emptied the glass and buzzed the waitress for another.

After the bourbon had come, he took Fratt's letter from the 'ducer and inserted Raspold's. On the screen of the visor he saw the living room of Raspold's apartment on the sixtieth level of the city of Denver. Raspold himself was not sitting down to face the screen. As nervous and energetic as Carmody, he found it difficult to sit for any length of time.

Raspold was a rapier clothed in flesh, a tall, very lean man with slick black hair, brown-black eyes as sharp and glittering as two tomahawks. He had a large bulbous nose, like a bloodhound's. He wore the scarlet coveralls and black neckruff of an employee of the Prometheus Interstellar Lines. Carmody was not surprised at this, for he had seen the detective in many disguises.

Raspold stopped pacing long enough to wave at Carmody and say, "Greetings, John, you old reprobate! Forgive me if this is a short letter."

He resumed walking back and forth, while he spoke loudly in his deep baritone. "I have to be off in a few minutes, and there's no telling how long I'll be on this particular scent. Also, the ship that'll be taking this letter is scheduled to leave in half an hour.

"John, while I was on this case—for which you see me dressed up—I accidentally learned of something irrelevant to the case, but very grave. Believe me, very grave. A group of rich and fanatical laymen, of your religion I'm sorry to say, have determined to assassinate Yess, the god of Kareen. None of their own members will be doing this, but they've hired an assassin, maybe several, to do the deed. He's one of the really big pros. I don't know his identity. But I believe the killer will be from Earth. Anyway, if the assassin is successful, or even if he fails and is caught, the repercussions will be bad.

"I can't do anything about this myself, because I'm tied up until this case can be completed. I've notified 3-E, and they'll undoubtedly send agents to Kareen. They'll also probably warn Yess. Then again, they may not, because they won't want it known that Earthmen are attempting this.

"But I think you might want to go yourself, take a hand in things. I say this because the killer may be a man who has gone through the Night, become an Algulist, and is therefore a thoroughly dangerous man. It'll take another Nighter to oppose him, and an Earth Nighter would understand him better. Of course, this being an Algulist is only a supposition, actually, a rumor. Maybe it's not even possible. I don't know enough about Kareen to be sure.

"If the killer hasn't been Nightized, he'll have to do his work before the Night starts. So he, and therefore you, don't have much time.

"Maybe you'll choose to ignore this. Maybe Yess is well able to take care of himself. However, here are the names of some potential assassins, top pros. You won't know any of them. All the big boys of the days of our youth are dead, imprisoned, lost, or, like yourself, transmogrified."

Raspold gave ten names, spelled them, and added a brief description of each man. He ended, "Good luck and my blessings to you, John. Next time you get to Earth, I hope I'll be there, too. It'll be nice to see your pleasantly ugly face again, and you can derive pleasure from gazing upon my noble Roman features and listening to my scintillating wit and enormous erudition. But as of now, I'm off! Tallyho!"

Carmody took the reader from his head and reached out for the second bourbon. Before touching it, his hand stopped. Now was not the time to get half-drunk. Not only did he have to consider Fratt—for all he knew Fratt might be on this ship—but he had an even more important problem. The cardinal should be informed of this turn of events. If what Raspold said was true—and he was usually reliable—then the Church was in even more danger than the cardinal had predicted. Assassination of Yess by members of the Church itself would cause an eruption that might be cataclysmic.

"The fools!" Carmody swore softly. "The blind hate-filled fools!"

He inserted two stanleys into a slot; a blank letter sheet issued from the hole beneath it. Carmody turned on the screen on the wall by the table, inserted the blank into the 'ducer, dropped three stanleys into its slot, and punched the DIC button. After dictating the letter to the cardinal, he called the waitress and asked her if the letter would be sent out to be shipped on the next vessel to Wildenwooly. She brought a charger for him to sign and fingerprint, since letters were very expensive and he did not have enough money on him to pay for it.

Carmody then went to the men's room and took an oxidizer to burn up the alcohol in his blood. The only other tenant was Abdu, the import-export businessman who had gotten on at Wildenwooly.

Abdu did not respond to Carmody's maneuvers to engage him in conversation. Beyond "Yeah," or "Is that so?" and several grunts, he was silent. Carmody gave up and returned to his seat in the passenger room.

He had been seated no more than ten minutes, his eyes half-shut and ignoring the movie on the screen, when he was interrupted.

"Father, is this seat taken?"

A young priest of the Jesuit order was standing by him,

smiling somewhat long-toothedly at him. Tall and thin, he had an ascetic face, light-blue eyes, dark hair, and a pale skin. His accent was Irish, and a moment later he identified himself as Father Paul O'Grady from Lower Dublin. He had served in the parish of Mexico City, Western Middle Level, for only a year after graduation from the seminary. Then he had been sent to Springboard to help with the situation there.

O'Grady was frank about his extreme nervousness. "I feel lost, not only from Earth but from myself. I seem to be breaking into many little pieces. I feel tiny, very tiny; everything seems so big."

"Hang on," Carmody said. He did not want to talk, but he could not ignore the poor young fellow. "Many people feel just as you do, about half the passengers in this ship, I'd bet. You want a drink? There's still time before take off."

O'Grady shook his head. "No. I don't want to depend upon a crutch."

"Crutch, hell!" Carmody said. "Don't be ridiculous, son. If you need it, you need it. This'll soon be over; your feet'll be on solid earth again and the blue skies, just like Earth's, will be over you. Stewardess!"

"You must think I'm an awful baby," O'Grady said.

"Yes, I do," Carmody replied. He chuckled as the young priest looked disconcerted. "But I don't think you're a coward. If you'd refused to go on after getting here, you would be. But you're not. So, you'll grow up."

O'Grady was silent for a while, chewing the cud of Carmody's remarks. He said, "By the way, I was so nervous I forgot to inquire your name, Father."

Carmody told him.

O'Grady's eyes widened. "You're not the Father Carmody who's the . . . the father of . . ."

"Say it."

"Of the false god Yess of Kareen?"

Carmody nodded.

"They say you're going on a mission to Kareen!" O'Grady burst out. "They say you're going to denounce Yess and expose Boontism as false!"

"Who's they?" Carmody said softly. "And keep your voice down."

"Oh, everybody knows," O'Grady said, waving his hand to indicate, apparently, the entire universe.

"The Vatican will be pleased to know how well their deepest secrets are kept," Carmody said. "Well, for your information, I am not going to Kareen to denounce Yess."

O'Grady seized Carmody's arm and said, "You're not going to renounce our faith for Boontism?"

Carmody pulled his arm away. "Is that another rumor?" he said coldly. "No. I'll admit there are some unsettling aspects about Boontism. But my faith is unshaken. Confused, perhaps, and questioning, but unshaken. And you may tell everybody that, also."

"We're having much trouble on Springboard," O'Grady said. "The number of our flock lost to Boontism is alarming. I'm not at liberty to tell even you how high the figure is, but I can say that it's alarming."

"You said it twice," Carmody replied.

"Father, perhaps you could stay long enough on Springboard to preach a while. We need a man such as you, a man who's been to Kareen and who can expose their so-called miracles and their so-called god as lies."

"I haven't time to stay," Carmody replied. "Moreover, I'd be a big disappointment to you. The so-called miracles are real, and whether or not Yess is a true savior of his planet is a question even the Holy Father himself does not care to answer. Not yet."

Carmody hitched himself forward, stared at the screen without seeing the figures upon it, and said, "I warn you that you had best keep quiet about meeting or about our conversation. This mission is supposed to be secret. Only myself and certain powers of the Church presumably know about it, although I can see that the grapevine has been busy again. It's the only thing in the universe faster than the speed of light. But if you breathe one word about this, you'll get an exceedingly severe reprimand and a check in your career that'll set you back twenty years. So keep your mouth shut!"

O'Grady blinked, and his face became both red and hurt. To Carmody's relief, the takeoff warning buzzed, and the captain began his pitch. The rest of the way to Springboard, O'Grady was too concerned with controlling his fear to talk.

When the *White Mule* had landed, Carmody decided to leave it for a while. He needed to stretch his legs, to look again at a place with which he had once more been familiar. It would also be the last "normal" planet he would see for some time.

The port had changed much in ten years, as had the city beyond it. The white Brobdingnagian cones fashioned by the almost extinct beavites—warm-blooded animals which emulated the termites of Earth in eating wood and constructing buildings of cementoid excrement—were still numerous. The first colonists had killed the beavites and moved into the ready-made skyscrapers. Then houses made of logs or artificial foamstone had filled in the places between the cones. But the original human constructions were all gone now, replaced by large structures of stone and plastic beams.

There were many more ships in the landing circles than when he had last been here. Carmody thanked God that he had been privileged to see the planets when they were relatively untouched by human beings. Not that there weren't many more to be discovered and explored yet. But his ways lately had been confined to much-trodden paths.

He walked around the buildings of the port for a half-hour, then went back to his terminus for the decontamination process. A large crowd in the main lobby barred his path. For a moment, he could not determine what was causing the angry shouts, red faces, threatening fists. Then he saw that a group, some of whom carried signs: *Christian Protective Society*, had surrounded a dozen men and women. These, aside from their defensive attitudes, seemed no different in appearance than their persecutors.

It was only when he managed to push through the crowd that he got close enough to see the broad gold rings on the index fingers of the besieged group. The rings were incised with a circle beneath which were two crossed phallic-looking spears. He had seen several of these on Wildenwooly and knew then that the attacked people were converts to Boontism. They were gathered by the customs desk and doing their best to ignore the taunts and insults howled at them. Facing the ranks of the Christian Protective Society was a beefy, thick-browed, big-nosed priest. Carmody recognized him at once, although he had not seen him in twelve years. He was Father Christopher Bakeling, and he had entered the priesthood and the Order of St. Jairus the same year as Carmody.

Carmody made his way toward him, the crowd dividing at sight of the clerical garments. Carmody placed himself between the giant priest and the Boontists.

"Father Bakeling, what's going on?"

Bakeling's eyes widened.

"John Carmody! What are you doing here?"

"Not making trouble, I can tell you that! What's your beef with those people?"

"Beef!" the giant priest shouted. "Beef! Carmody, I know you well! You're here to make trouble, sure as 'Needlenose' is your nickname!"

He waved his arms and sputtered for a moment, then succeeded in gaining self-control. He pointed at a tall handsome man standing at the admission desk.

"See him! That's Father Gideon! He became a worshiper of the foul idol Boonta, and now he's taking three of his own parish with him, to Hell! And what's more, two of my own flock!"

A woman in the crowd yelled, "Gideon's an anti-Christ, that's what he is, an anti-Christ! And him my own confessor! He ought to be put in jail and locked up where he can't go spilling all his secrets."

"He ought to be stoned!" Bakeling cried. "Stoned! Or hung in a field, like Judas! He's betrayed his own sweet Lord for a devil, and he's lured . . ."

"Shut up, Bakeling," Carmody said harshly. "You're making a bad situation worse by your big mouth and public antics! I'd think you'd want to keep this quiet. This kind of advertisement for them, and for us, is best avoided."

Bakeling, his fists clenched, thrust himself against Carmody and forced the little priest back. "You taking their side? I know you, Carmody! You aren't free of the Boontist taint, yourself! I've even heard that you fornicated with the priestess of Boonta or did something equally wicked, and that the son of Boonta is also your son! I didn't believe it; no man of the cloth could be so evil, not even a freak like you! But now I'm not so sure!"

"Get away from me, Bakeling," Carmody said. He felt anger rising like mercury in a heat wave. "Back away, and try to act like a man of God!"

He paused, then could hold his anger no longer. "Don't push me! I'm warning you!"

"Ah, you banty rooster, you believe your own reputation for being a dangerous man! You're too little for me to even spit on! And not good enough for me to spit on, either!"

The woman who had denounced Gideon spoke out again. "What kind of a priest are you? Taking up sides against your own religion, your own people?"

Carmody attempted to calm himself. In a lower voice, he said, "I am trying to do the Christian thing, trying to keep you people from acting with hate. Remember: Love thy enemy."

The woman screamed, "Next you'll be telling us to turn our other cheek and invite that filth to dinner! They're evil, Father, evil! And that Father Gideon is Satan himself! How could he . . . how could he . . . ?" And she burst into a string of oaths and invective that Carmody in his former days, would have admired. Whatever else possessed the woman, she certainly had imagination and a flair for the profane.

"Out of my way, Carmody!" the huge priest bellowed. "I'm going to make Gideon recant if I have to wring his neck!"

"This isn't the way to do it!" Carmody said.

"The hell it isn't!" Bakeling shouted, and he swung at Carmody. As the little priest ducked under the ponderous fist, the anger and frustration that had been burning in him since Anna's death took over. He rammed the stiffened fingers of his left hand into the big soft belly before him. Bakeling clutched at his stomach, whooshed, bent over and was hit squarely in the nose with a fist. Blood spurted out over his shoes onto Carmody's legs.

A single roar welled from the crowd. They surged forward, drove Carmody back by the wall of their bodies, and pressed him against the screaming and yelling Boontists. Police whistles blew. Several fists struck Carmody, and he lost consciousness.

When he opened his eyes, his head, jaw, ribs and shoulders hurt. He was being administered to by a policeman in the white-and-black uniform and cone-shaped hat of the Springboard city force. Before Carmody could say anything, he was jerked upright and carried along by two big men toward the lobby and outdoors. Here several paddy wagons were waiting for him and for the other rioters who had not been swift enough or had been too injured to run.

However, he was given special treatment. While most of the others were forced into the wagons, he was urged ungently into the back seat of a patrol car. A lieutenant sat on one side of him. On the other was Father Bakeling, a handkerchief pressed to his nose.

"Now see what you've done, you troublemaker!" Bakeling mumbled. "You started a riot, and you've disgraced your Church and your vicarship!"

"I?"

Carmody looked startled, then he started to laugh but quit when his ribs wrenched a groan from him. "Are we going to be booked?" he said to the lieutenant.

"Father Bakeling is pressing charges against you." He handed the priest a wristphone. "You are entitled to one call to your lawyer."

Carmody ignored him and spoke to Bakeling, "If I'm delayed so long I miss getting a ship to Kareen, you'll have to

93

answer to the highest authority for it. And I mean the highest."

Bakeling dabbed at his nose with his handkerchief and growled, "Don't threaten me, Carmody. Remember, I know you for what you are, a lying little trickster."

"I'll make a call after all," Carmody said. He took the phone. "What's the anticode?"

The lieutenant told him the numbers, and Carmody repeated them. The gray half-moon on the upper half of the 5.08-centimeter disc became luminous.

"What's Bishop Emzaba's number?"

Bakeling started; the lieutenant's eyes blinked. Bakeling said, "I won't tell you."

"All right, lieutenant, *you* tell me."

The policeman sighed, but he pulled a little book from his beltbag and leafed through it. "606."

Carmody spoke the number, and a second later the face of a young priest appeared on the tiny screen. Carmody rotated the movable upper part of the disc, and the face seemed to spring out of the screen and to hang, much enlarged, sixteen centimeters in front of the disc.

"Father Carmody of Wildenwooly speaking. I must speak to the bishop. At once. It's an emergency."

The face thinned away; the screen became blank, although it still glowed. Abruptly, the features of a mulatto danced before Carmody. The shimmering face scowled, and the deep voice was harsh. "Carmody? What kind of a mess are you in now?"

"One not entirely my own fault, Your Lordship," Carmody said. "As a matter of fact, I was merely trying to effect some Christian action, not to mention Christian charity. But I failed. And here I am, on my way to the police station, about to be charged and booked."

"I heard about the action at the spaceport and about your being involved," Embaza said. "I've already started some action of my own. It may not be Christian, but it's a matter of utmost necessity."

Carmody turned the phone so that the bishop could see Bakeling.

Emzaba's scowl deepened. "Bakeling! Is it true you were fighting with another priest? And that you were leading a mob of your own parishioners against the Boontist converts?"

Bakeling stuttered for a moment, then said, "I was merely trying to make Father Gideon and his people see the error of their ways, Your Lordship! But this, this Needlenose here, stood up for them! He actually attacked me, a brother priest, a member of his own order, to protect the Boontist heretics!"

"Is that true?" Embaza said. "Carmody, turn the phone so I can see your face!"

Carmody twisted the phone and said, "It's a long story, Your Lordship, and it would take a long time to separate the various threads of truth from those of passion. But I don't have time to explain. I must be on my way to Kareen! Immediately! I am on a mission of the gravest importance, authorized by the Holy Father himself!"

Embaza said, "Yes, I know. A courier came yesterday to inform me I must help to speed you on your way, no matter how unreasonable or strange the demands you might make. I understand something of your mission, and I am prepared to aid you. But, Carmody, a brawl! You should realize more than anybody how necessary it is that you get involved in nothing which will delay you!"

"I do, and I'm sorry. But here I am. Now, how do I get back to the port in time to catch the *White Mule* before it takes off? Or do I?"

Embaza asked to speak to the lieutenant. Carmody swiveled the phone so that the policeman and bishop could talk face to face. The lieutenant listed the charges that were to be made against Carmody. At these, the bishop frowned so fiercely that he looked like one of the ebony idols fashioned by his ancestors in the long ago.

"I'll speak to you again, lieutenant. Or someone will," Embaza said.

His face dissolved, but the ghost of his anger hung in the air. Bakeling shifted uneasily, glancing sideways now and then at Carmody. "If you get out of this, you slimy little rat, and I'm unjustly placed in the wrong . . . if I have to suffer because of you . . . so help me, I'll—"

"You'll what?" Carmody said. "Refuse to learn your lesson and go charging off like a bull in rut and batter your thick head against the wall again?"

"You're filthy, Carmody, a reproach to your sacred office."

"Strong situations demand strong language," Carmody said. "But didn't you know that the bishop would be very angry with you because you were making martyrs of the Boontists? That is the one thing the Church does not want to do, and that was the one thing you were doing."

"I was acting by the dictates of my conscience," Bakeling said stiffly.

"You better take your conscience out and polish it up a

little," Carmody said. "Make it shine like a mirror, and take a good look at yourself in it. I'll admit the sight will be nauseating, but sometimes it takes sickness to make a man well."

"You mealy-mouthed little hypocrite!"

Carmody's only reply was a shrug. He was beginning to get depressed again, for he knew that the bishop was right.

The car stopped before the precinct headquarters. This was in one of the beavite cones taken over by the early settlers, a structure grayish-white on the outside, with a diameter of one hundred meters at the base and towering to four hundred at the apex. Once the cone had housed the entire central police organization of the planet. But in the fifty years of its colonization, Springboard had gained such a population that the building now was only the base for the first precinct. The planetary base had been shifted to a new structure twenty kilometers away, a skyscraper built by men.

The original entrance, once just large enough for two beavites to pass through shoulder to shoulder, had been cut away to make a huge arch. Carmody went through the arch with the lieutenant and Bakeling into a long and high-ceilinged hall, the white nakedness of which had been covered with green formite. The hall led them to a big room. There was a curious smell, compounded of the fifty-year-old traces of beavite odor and the immemorial effluvium of police buildings and courthouses: cigar smoke and urine. Under the green paint, Carmody knew, were splotches and streaks of blood, for the beavites had refused to be dispossessed peacefully.

Carmody and Bakeling sat down on a bench while the lieutenant left to talk to his superiors. Five minutes later, he returned, his face pale and lips tight.

"The bishop has interfered with police procedure!" he said. "He must really be swinging his weight around. I just got word to drop all charges and release you two. And as if that isn't bad enough, I'm to escort you, Carmody, back to the port."

The two priests, silent, rose and followed him out of the building. This time, Carmody was put into an aircar. The craft rose upward and then rushed toward the spires of the port, its sirens wailing and its yellow lights flashing.

The lieutenant, sitting in the seat before Carmody, suddenly turned and handed him the phone. "The bishop," he said, and turned his back.

Emzaba's face shot up from the screen, and stopped only

a few centimeters from Carmody's. He was so close that the priest could perceive the writhing lines that formed the projection. They added to the wrathful thunder of the bishop's words.

Afterward, Carmody, thoroughly chastened and contrite, apologized. He said nothing about the death of his wife. But the bishop must have heard of it, for, immediately after his lecture, he softened.

"I know that you are carrying a grievous burden, John. Under ordinary circumstances, I would have withheld a tongue-lashing. But nothing should have diverted you from your mission."

"Things have a way of getting out of hand," Carmody said. "Well, I'll be on Kareen soon and fully engaged in my task."

The bishop was silent for a minute, then he said, "Would it be presumptuous to ask for more details of your mission? I have a general idea, but I was not given any specifics. However, don't feel that you have to tell me anything just because I'm curious. Regard me as a fellow religionist who's gravely concerned and who can keep his mouth shut."

Carmody delayed to light a cigarette, then said, "I can tell Your Lordship that my mission is twofold. One, I'm to try to talk Yess out of sending his missionaries to extra-Kareenan planets. Two, I will also try to talk Yess out of forcing the entire population of Kareen into going through the Night of Light."

Emzaba was shocked. "I did not know that Yess intended to keep all his worshippers Awake!"

"It's not definite. Apparently, he's still considering it and won't give his decision until just before the Night begins."

"But why should he do that?"

"I was told that he would like to weed out all the secret worshipers of Algul and also the lukewarms and the lip-servers. He wants a planetful of zealots."

The bishop nodded. "And Yess would send these fanatics out as missionaries, right?"

"Right."

"And Yess has the power to do this, to make everybody put himself into the terrible jeopardy of the Night?"

"He has the power."

The bishop hesitated, frowned, then said, "Our superiors must believe that you have some chance of succeeding. Otherwise, you'd not have been sent to Yess."

"They could also be doing it out of desperation," Carmody

said. "The inroads that Boontism has been making into our faith, into all non-Kareenan faiths, have been devastating. And it will get worse."

"I know. Yet . . . you went through the Night . . . it is even said that you were one of the Fathers of Yess . . . but you did not become a worshiper of the Goddess. So, there is hope. But I do not understand why you have not been publicized by the Church. You are our greatest living testimony to our faith."

Carmody smiled grimly and said, "There is great danger in my testifying. How would it look to the average man if I had to swear—and I would have to—that the phenomena of the Night are real? That the god Yess is formed out of the air by a mystical union between the Great Mother and the Seven Fathers? That so-called miracles are a dime a dozen on Kareen, that Boontism can offer living proof of its claims, solid and visual results from the practice of its religion?

"Or that I was a criminal of the worst sort, a murderer many times, a thief, a pervert, you name it—yet after I passed through the Night I did not even have to be given the rehabilitation treatment at Johns Hopkins?"

"They would say that Boontism did it and would give even more credence to the Kareenan missionaries. Yet, you did not become a worshiper of Boonta."

"I might have if I had stayed on Kareen," Carmody said. "But I returned almost immediately to Earth after the Night. And while in Hopkins, I had an experience the details of which I won't go into now. It's enough that I decided to join the Church, and became a lay brother and am now a priest."

The bishop said, "I still don't understand. You affirm the validity of Yess and of Boonta, yet you also declare the truth of our faith. How can you reconcile such opposites?"

Carmody shrugged and said, "I don't. I have my questions, plenty of them. But so far they've not been answered. Perhaps this visit to Kareen will do it."

The aircar settled down in the parking lot. Carmody said goodby to Embaza, received his blessing, then delayed to ask the bishop to go easy on Bakeling. Emzaba replied that he would try to be as just as possible. But before he was through, he would make Bakeling understand just what he had done and promise to avoid such errors in the future.

Carmody got into his seat in the *White Mule* only a minute before the ports were shut for the pre-takeoff checkout.

He saw that most of the Boontist converts involved in the riot had been able to make the ship.

One fellow, who had entered on Carmody's heels, was not a Boontist. He was a short muscular man who looked as if he were about Carmody's physicological age, that is, anywhere between thirty-five and a hundred. He had thick, black, very curly hair, a broad Amerindian face with a big aquiline nose, thin lips, and a jutting cleft chin. He wore all-white clothing: a conical hat with a broad flappy brim, a close-fitting shirt with puffy sleeves, a big leatheroid belt with a hexagonal metal buckle, a white beltbag, and trousers that clung to the thighs but ballooned from the lower legs. His shoes lacked the fashionable frills and festoons of spherelets; they were simple and rugged.

Clutched in one hand was a large white-covered book. On its cover, in the old-style nonphonemic alphabet, were words in black: TRUE VERSION—HOLY SCRIPTURES. By this and his white garments, Carmody knew the man belonged to an increasingly powerful religious group. The members of the Rockbottom Church of God—sometimes referred to by their enemies as the Hardasses—were fundamentalists who believed they had returned to the original faith of the original Christians. Carmody had met a few on Wildenwooly.

However, it was not the man's religion that made Carmody's eyes open wide. It was the shock of recognition.

So, all the old pros were not gone! This man was Al Lieftin, and he had once worked with Carmody during a phase of the Staronif robbery.

Lieftin's own eyes expanded on seeing Carmody's face. They opened even more when they lowered to take in the maroon robes of a priest of the Order of St. Jairus.

Lieftin raised his hand as if to ward off something, took a step backward, then turned away. But the priest called to him.

"Al Lieftin! Come sit by me! No need to avoid me. I've nothing to hide. And it looks as if we've both changed."

Lieftin hesitated. The color came back to his face; he grinned, and he almost swaggered over to the seat beside Carmody's.

"You startled me," he said. "It's been so many years. You . . . you're Father Carmody now?"

"Father it is," said Carmody. "And you?"

"I'm a diaconus of the True Church," Lieftin said. "Praise the Lord! The evil days are gone forever; I saw the light in time. I repented, I paid for my sins. And now I preach the Basic Word."

"I'm very happy that you're at peace," Carmody said. "At least, I presume you are. We've taken somewhat different paths, but they are both, I trust, good paths, the right paths.

"Tell me," Father Carmody continued, that is if you don't object, why're you going to Dante's Joy? The Night of Light is due. Surely you're not planning to go through it?"

"Never! No, I'm going because my church has sent me to make a report on the pre-Night rituals, then take the last ship out. I preferred not to have to watch those Satanic doings, but the Eldest himself asked me if I would."

"Why does your church want a report? Certainly, there are enough data about Kareen in the Earth libraries."

Lieftin said, "The bitter truth is that we've lost more people to the false god Yess than we care to admit. Many men and women I would never have believe could be persuaded from the Basic Word have succumbed to the Satanic wiles of the Kareenan missionaries.

"So, I'm to make a detailed report, find things that the books don't report, get a first-hand account. I'm to take films, too, and use all this for lecture tours on Earth. I'll show the people of Earth what sinners the Kareenans really are. When the indescribably obscene evil acts the Kareenans commit in the name of their religion are shown, why, then, the Terrestrials won't be so full of fire to convert to Boontism. They will have seen for themselves what abominations are practiced in Boonta's name."

Carmody did not tell Lieftin that this approach had been tried more than once. Sometimes, it worked. But often it had just the opposite effect. It aroused curiosity, even desire.

Carmody lit a cigarette. Lieftin sniffed. Carmody said, "You used to chain-smoke. Was it hard for you to give up the habit?"

"No, praise the Lord. I never felt a moment's temptation from the instant I saw the light. Never! I gave up the evils of tobacco, alcohol and fornication. And I thank the Lord that He has shielded me from all temptation since."

"Tobacco and alcohol can be evil if their use is abused," Carmody said. "But moderation is a virtue, too. Usually, anyway."

"Don't you believe it, Carmody. When fighting evil, it's all or none."

He hesitated, then said, "By the way, maybe I should not bring up the old days. But whatever happened to the

Staronif? I remember we all had to take off that night. I just barely escaped the guards and their wego. I heard later that Raspold almost caught you, but you tricked him. I never did hear what happened to the Staronif. You get away with it?"

"I escaped from Raspold because he was treed by a lugar," Carmody said, referring to the huge felinoid carnivore of the planet of Tulgey. "I almost made it back to our ship, but then I got treed, too. The lugar was coming up after me; don't believe those stories about their being too big to climb trees. I had only one weapon because I'd emptied all my ammo clips during the running battle with the guards. That weapon was the Staronif.

"I shoved it down the lugar's throat, and it swallowed the Staronif. The last I saw of the lugar, it was running through the forest, screaming as if it had the grandfather of all bellyaches."

"God!" Lieftin said. Then, "Sorry. I didn't mean to use the Lord's name in vain. But the Staronif! Ten million giffords lost in a cat's stomach. What a fortune you could have made! And all those months of planning and all that money you spent getting things set up!"

Carmody chuckled and said, "It didn't seem funny then. Now, I laugh about it. Somewhere in that big dark forest, the most valuable jewel in the Galaxy lies inside the skeleton of a lugar."

Lieftin wiped his forehead with a handkerchief he took from his sleeve. Carmody looked at it, for he wondered if the handkerchief still had the little steel ball sewed in one corner. Lieftin had been famous once for snapping it in a man's eye during a fight and often removing the eye. Now, there was no sign of it.

The stewardess announced takeoff. Ten minutes later, ship's time, the *White Mule* was in the atmosphere of Kareen. In another ten minutes, it had landed in the light of the late afternoon sun.

Again Carmody went through inspection. He lost sight of Lieftin until he was on the way to the exit from the spaceport. As he passed the door to the washroom (designed for male bipeds of non-Kareenan origin), the door swung open. And he saw Lieftin stubbing out a cigarette in an ashtray.

Lieftin looked up at the same time. He started, then charged out and seized Carmody's arm.

"Forgive me, Carmody, I lied to you. I do feel temptation now and then. But I usually fight it off with the Lord's

101

help. Only, this time, I fell. Maybe because this trip is making me very nervous. You know, coming to a place so besotted with evil."

"This place is no more evil than any other place," Carmody said. "Don't worry. I don't judge you. I won't laugh at you or tell anybody about this. Forget about it. Excuse me. I think the official delegates are about to greet me."

He had seen his old friend Tand enter the main room. Tand did not look much older than when he had last seen him. There were a few gray streaks in the feathery hair of his head, and he looked a little heavier than Carmody remembered him. But he was the same happy-looking fellow, his blue-tinged teeth showing in a grin. Nor had his present important position changed his manner of dress. He still wore inexpensive and conservative clothes.

Tand strode toward him, his arms out and called, "John Carmody! Welcome!"

They embraced. Tand said, in English, "How are you, Father?"

He grinned, and Carmody knew that Tand was using the title in a double sense.

"I'm fine," Carmody replied in Kareenan. "And you, Father Tand?"

He used the word *pwelch*, which was reserved for a Father of Yess.

Tand stepped back and said, "I'm as happy as can be under the present conditions. Oh . . ." He turned to the other Kareenans, behind him. "Allow me to introduce . . ."

Carmody greeted each with the formal combination of handshake and dipping of both knees. The four were members of the government: a secret-police official, a priest, an enthnologist, and a secretary of the head of the world state.

All seemed interested in what had brought Carmody back to their planet. Abog, the secretary of Rilg, the state head, was a young man, very personable, but he had something in his bearing—or was it his voice?—that Carmody mistrusted.

Abog said, "We were hoping that you had come to announce your conversion to Boontism."

"I have come to talk to Yess," Carmody said.

Tand took charge. "Would you like to go now to your hotel room? Inasmuch as you are one of the Seven, the government has reserved one of the best suites. At state expense, of course."

Tand suggested to the others that they must be very busy.

102

They took the hint and said goodby. But Abog, before leaving, insisted that Carmody give him an appointment, that very evening, if possible. The priest replied that he would be happy to talk to him.

After the officials had left, Tand conducted Carmody to his car. The vehicle was a low-graviton unit, as were most of those on the street.

"Change," Tand said. "It's everywhere in the universe, even on our off-the-beaten-path planet. Population has quadrupled. New industries, founded on Federation technology and sometimes on Federation loans, have sprung up by the thousands."

Tand drove; Carmody looked out the window. The massive stone structures with the carved grinning or snarling faces were as before. There were more people in the streets, and they wore clothes of a style definitely influenced by Federation garments.

"The city you know," Tand said, "is about the same. But around it, covering what used to be farmlands or woods, is a great new city. It's not made of stone, not made to last. Too many people too soon. We can no longer afford to take our time in building."

"It's like that everywhere," Carmody replied. "Tell me, are you still connected with the police?"

"No more. But I have influence. Any Father has. Why?"

"A man named Al Lieftin came in on the *White Mule* with me. Years ago, he was a hired killer. He's traveling under his own name now, so I presume he was mogrified at Hopkins or a similar institution. He claims now to be a diaconus of the Rockbottom Church of God. His story may be true. If we had time, we could check on him. But we don't. And there's a possibility he may be the assassin sent by Earth fanatics to kill Yess. You know of that, don't you?"

"I've heard. I'll put the police on Lieftin's trail. But they'll have a hard time keeping an eye on him, unless they place him under house arrest. Once he's out in the pre-Night festival crowds, he can easily give them the slip. Or disappear without trying."

"What're the chances of house arrest?"

"None at all. He could kick up too much of a fuss. The authorities don't want to offend a Federation citizen unless they have a very good reason."

Carmody was silent for a while. Then he said, "There is another man whom I would like watched. But I hesitate

103

to say anything about him. This is such a personal thing, big for me but little in comparison with the plot against Yess."

He told his friend about the threats from the man who called himself Fratt. Tand was thoughtful. Finally, he said, "You think the Earthman Abdu could be Fratt?"

"Possibly but not very probably. The time element is against it. How would he have learned of my sudden decision to come here?"

"The explanation might be very easy if you knew what he did. I'll have someone shadow him. The police will be too busy with the crowds to spare anybody. But I'll get a private operative."

Tand stopped the car in front of their destination. The Kareenan equivalent of a bellhop loaded Carmody's baggage on a graviton sled, and the two proceeded straight to Carmody's suite. Since Tand had made arrangements, there was no registration to go through. But a group of reporters tried to interview Carmody. Tand waved them away. Even though they were as aggressive as their Terrestrial counterparts, they obeyed Tand, a Father of Yess.

Where once the two would have had to walk up great curving flights of stairs, they now shot up in a graviton cage. So wide were the stairwells, it had not been necessary to cut into the stairs to make space for elevator shafts.

"This building has always been a hotel," Tand said. "It may be the oldest hotel in the universe. It was built more than five thousand years ago."

He spoke with pride. "It has been occupied so long that it is said a man with a keen nose may detect the odor of flesh, absorbed by the stones during the ages of habitation."

The cage stopped at the seventh floor, a lucky number and also chosen to honor Carmody as one of the Seven Fathers. His room was nearly two hectometers down the broad stone-walled corridor. The doors to the rooms were of iron, almost bank vault thick. Like many Kareenan doors, they were not hinged on one side but pivoted on pins in the middle. So secure were the rooms behind the doors, the occupants stayed inside during their Sleep instead of going into the mass vaults provided by the government.

Carmody investigated his three-room suite. The beds were carved out from the wall blocks, and the tables were fashioned from granite projections of the floor blocks.

"They don't build like this any more," Tand said with a shade of sadness. He poured out some thick dark-red wine into two multifaceted cups of white-and-red veined wood. The wine descended slowly as if it were molten granite itself.

"To your health, John."

"To yours. And to good men and women everywhere, whatever their form, and to the redemption of the lost, and God bless the children."

He drank and found the liquor was not sweet, as he had expected. It was very close to being bitter. Somehow, it did not become so. Instead, the tang became very pleasurable, and a glow spread through him and then, seemingly, out from him. The duskiness of the room became golden.

Tand offered him another cup. Carmody refused with thanks. "I want to see Yess. How soon before I can?"

Tand smiled. "You haven't changed your impetuousness. Yess is just as eager to see you as you are to see him. But he has many duties; being a god doesn't exempt him from the labors of a mortal. I'll go see him—his secretary, rather—and make an appointment."

"Whenever he wants," Carmody said. He chuckled. "Although it doesn't show much filial piety for a son to keep his long-absent Father waiting."

"You are thrice welcome, John. However, your presence is a little embarrassing—or could be. You see, the populace know *of* you but not much *about* you. Very few have heard about your not being a worshiper of Boonta. When this becomes general knowledge, it could create much doubt and confusion in the simple-minded. Even in the more sophisticated. How could a Father not be one of Boonta's faithful?"

"My own Church has asked me that. And I do not know. I've seen dozens of so-called miracles here, enough to stagger sextillions of infidels. Surely enough to convince the hardest-headed materialist. But I had no desire to convert.

"As a matter of fact, though I was not an atheist when I left Kareen for Earth, I had no inclination for any particular religion. While I was in Hopkins, I had a very strange— and essentially inexplicable—experience. It was this that led me into the Church. But I forgot. I wrote you about that."

Tand rose from his chair and said, "I'm off to see Yess. I'll phone you later."

He kissed the priest and left.

Carmody unpacked and then bathed in a tub the interior of which had been worn deep by friction from five millenia of running water and sliding flesh. He had no sooner dressed than the huge iron knocker on the door clanged. He freed the bolt and began to open the door, pushing on one side to let it swing outward. Though massive, the door was perfectly balanced and revolved as lightly as a ballerina on tiptoes.

Carmody stepped back and raised his hand to stop the inward-swinging half. At the same time, the Kareenan male in the hallway dipped his hand into his open beltbag. Carmody did not wait. Old reflexes took over. He jumped forward, hurled himself against the side of the door moving out into the hall. The Kareenan, drawing the automatic from the bag, had started to enter on the inward-swinging side. Apparently, he had intended to run in and shoot Carmody. He must have hoped to be concealed long enough by the door to confuse his victim.

Instead, the other side of the door was impelled by Carmody's shoulder driving against it. The entire assembly swung around much more swiftly than the assassin had planned. And the right-hand side came around and caught him as he recovered and turned. The weight sent him staggering backward. Carmody saw his look of surprise before the door, making a complete rotation, lost its momentum and closed the entrance again.

Then, the door swung out again as the Kareenan inside the room lunged at it, probably in a fury or panic to get to his man before he ran down the hallway. Carmody knew he could not run fast enough to reach the distant corner before the Kareenan got out. The hall was deserted, and there were no other doors open for him to take refuge behind.

He leaped in after the in-swinging section of door. He heard a yelp of surprise and rage. Swiftly, Carmody stopped the door and shot the bolt. He was safe, for the moment, anyway. He ran to the phone and called the desk clerk. Within a minute, the hotel police were outside his door. The assassin, of course, was gone.

Carmody answered questions of the police, and, a little later, of the city police. No, he did not know the Kareenan. Yes, he had been threatened by a man named Fratt. Carmody described the letter from him and said that Tand had already promised to take care of the matter.

The police left, but two guards were posted outside the door. It was unthinkable that a Father should be exposed to attack, now it was known his life was in danger. Carmody did not care for the guards because they would hamper his movements. However, he did not think he would have much trouble in losing them.

While he calmed his nerves with another cup of wine, he puzzled. Had the Kareenan been hired by Fratt? It did not seem very likely. Fratt would want a personal revenge; his own hand would have to inflict whatever torture of death he was planning.

He wondered about Lieftin. If the man was not what he seemed to be, if his diaconus speech and appearance were a disguise, if he were the assassin hired by the Earth fanatics, he might want to kidnap Carmody. He might hope to get some information from Carmody about Yess.

Carmody finished the wine and began pacing back and forth. He was not able to leave his room because he did not want to miss a call from Tand, but it made him nervous to wait.

His phone rang. He passed his hand over the screen, and it came alive. Abog, secretary to the world government head, looked out at him.

"I'm a little early, Father. But I'm very eager to talk to you. May I come up?"

Carmody consented. A few minutes later, the knocker clanged. Carmody opened the door a trifle and peeked out. The guards must have been impressed by Abog's splendid clothes and his credentials, for they were rigid with attention.

The secretary entered, and, immediately thereafter, the phone rang again. This time, an Earthman's face was on the screen.

"Job Gilson," he said in English. "ETS. I was told you wanted to see me."

Gilson was a man of middle age. He had a fair, lightly freckled complexion and brown hair. His features were so regular they made no impression. It was an easily forgotten face—valuable for an agent of Extra-Terrestrial Security.

"Can you wait? I have a visitor."

"I'm used to waiting," Gilson said. He smiled. "Just a glorified flatfoot."

Carmody passed his hand over the screen, and it went brown. He offered Abog a drink; the Kareenan accepted.

"Normally, I wouldn't rush into this," Abog said. "Unfortunately, time does not permit the usual diplomatic delays. So, I won't offend the Father if I come to the point?"

"On the contrary. You'd offend me if you slithered around

107

like a snake on oil, that is to say, like a politician. I like directness."

"Very well. However, you should know something first about the extent of the authority vested in me. Also, something about our governmental structure, and about the man at its head. I think . . ."

"I think your good intentions about going straight to the heart of the matter are being betrayed by your training. Never mind all the extraneous stuff."

Abog looked upset, but he rallied with a quick show of bluish teeth. "All right. The only thing is, I wanted you to realize that my government would never pry into your personal life or your beliefs—not at any other time, that is. Now, we must ask . . ."

"Ask."

Abog sucked in a deep breath, then said, "Have you or have you not come to announce your conversion to Boontism?"

"Is that all? No, I am not converting. I am firm in my faith."

"Oh."

Abog seemed disappointed. After a silence and a long stare past Carmody, he said, "Perhaps, you could use your influence as a Father to, uh, well, dissuade Yess."

"I don't know that I have any influence. Dissuade him from what?"

"Frankly, my chief, Rilg, is worried. If Yess makes the decision that all stay Awake, the effect will be catastrophic. Those who survive may be 'good,' 'purified,' but how many will live through the Night? The statisticians predict that over three-fourths of the population will die. Think of that, Father. Three-fourths! Kareenan civilization will be wiped out."

"Does Yess know this?"

"He has been told. He agrees that the statisticians may be correct. But he doesn't think they have to be. He maintains that there is a good reason why Yess usually triumphs over Algul during the Night. The majority of the Sleepers are, quote, good, unquote. Their dreaming state reflects their true desires. And these desires somehow affect those who stay Awake. Therefore, Yess wins.

"Following this reasoning, if all stay Awake, the effect will be the same as if most Slept. Only, the essentially 'good' will have a chance to be thoroughly purified of the evil elements present even in the best."

"He could be right," Carmody said.

"Yess could also be very wrong. We think he is. But even if he is right, think of what will happen! Even if the predictions are wrong, at least a fourth would be killed. What a devastation, what a slaughter! Men, women, children!"

"It does seem frightful."

"Frightful! It's hideous, savage! Why, even Algul could not think of anything so fiendish! If I did not know better, I would say . . ."

He stopped, rose, and moved close to the Earthman. He whispered, "There have been rumors that it was not really Yess who was born during that Night. It was Algul. But Algul, clever as he is, claimed to be Yess. Such a trick would be just like the Deceiver."

Carmody smiled and said, "You can't be serious?"

"Of course not. Do you think I'm one of those poor fools? But this kind of rumor shows the people's confusion. They can't understand how their great and kind god could require them to do this."

"Your scriptures predict just such an event."

Abog looked frightened, and there was panic in his voice.

"True, but nobody ever expected it to happen. Only a handful of the superorthodox believed in it, even prayed for it."

"There's something I don't understand," Carmody said. "What would happen to those who just refused to go through the Night?"

"Anybody who refuses to obey an order of Yess is automatically and legally classified as a follower of Algul. He can be arrested and imprisoned."

"But he still won't have to undergo the Night?"

"Oh, yes, he will. He'll not be given the drugs to put him Asleep, and he'll have to face whatever comes, in a prison cell."

"But suppose there's a mass resistance? The government wouldn't have time or the facilities to deal with a large body of people, would they?"

"You don't understand Kareenans. No matter how frightened they will be, the majority would find it unthinkable to disobey Yess."

The more Carmody thought about it, the less he liked it. To some extent, he could understand the men and women being forced to go through with it, but the children! The innocents would suffer; most of them would die. If a parent hated his child, consciously or unconsciously, he would kill the child. And those parents who were defending their children against the attacks of others might be killed, and then the children would die, too.

"I don't understand it," he said. "But then I am not, as you pointed out, a Kareenan."

"But will you try to persuade him not to force this?"

"Have you talked to the other Fathers?"

"Some of them," Abog said. "I got nowhere. They will go along with whatever Yess wants."

Carmody was silent for a while. He fully intended to argue with Yess, but he was not sure that it would be wise to tell Abog so. Who knew what capital Abog and the party he represented might make of his statement? Or what resentment Yess might have if Carmody's intentions were published?

"I'll just have to take the consequences," Carmody said aloud. "All right, I do mean to talk Yess out of making the decision you and so many others fear. But I do not want to be quoted on TV or have this interview printed in the papers. If such happens, I'll deny everything."

Abog seemed happy. Smiling, he said, "Very good. Perhaps you can succeed where others have failed. So far, he has made no official pronouncement. There's time yet."

He thanked Carmody and left.

The priest called Gilson back and told him to come up; then he notified the guards to let the Earthman in when he came.

The phone rang a third time. Tand's face appeared on the screen.

"I'm sorry, John. Yess can't see you tonight. But he will see you tomorrow night at the Temple. Meanwhile, what do you intend to do to pass the time?"

"I think I'll put on a mask and join the merrymakers in the street."

"You can, because you're a Father," Tand said. "But your Earth compatriots, those men you spoke about, Lieftin and Abdu, they can't. I got the police to restrict them to the hotel unless they agree to go through the Night. As a matter of fact, all non-Kareenans are restricted by the new ruling. I'm afraid there'll be a lot of disgruntled tourists and scientists tonight. But that's the way it is."

"You swing a lot of weight, Tand."

"I don't overuse my power. But I think this ruling is a good idea. I'd like to go out with you, John, but I'm tied up with too many official duties. Power brings its responsibilities, you know."

"I know. Good night, Tand."

His hand passed over the screen, and he turned to walk away. The phone rang. This time, it was not a face but a hideous mask that appeared on the screen. The mask blocked out all view of what lay behind it. From the noises Carmody surmised that the phone was in a public booth on one of the main streets.

The voice that issued from the stiff lips of the mask was distorted.

"Carmody, this is Fratt. I just wanted to get a good look at you before you died. I want to see if you're suffering, although you could not possibly suffer as much as my son and I did."

The priest forced himself to be calm. In an even voice he said, "Fratt, I don't even know you. I can't even remember the incident you allege took place. So, why don't you come up to my room and talk to me? Maybe you'll change your mind."

There was a pause so long that Carmody decided he had shocked Fratt. Then, "You don't think I'd be fool enough to put myself again in the power of a man like you? You must be insane!"

"All right. You name the time and place. I'll come alone to meet you; we'll talk this thing out."

"Oh, you'll meet me all right. But it'll be when and where you'll least expect it. At least, I've got you sweating. And begging."

A glove shaped like a claw moved up before the mask, and the screen went blank. Carmody went to the door in answer to the clanging of the knocker. Gilson entered.

Angrily, he said, "I'm afraid I won't be able to help you much, Father. I've just been notified that I'm restricted to the hotel."

"That's my fault," the bishop said. He told Gilson what had happened, but Gilson did not seem any happier, especially after he heard Carmody's account of the phone conversation with Fratt.

"I might as well take the next ship out," he said.

"Let's go down to the hotel dining room and eat," Carmody said. "It's on me. And I understand that the hotel has an Earth cook for those who can't adapt themselves to a Kareenan diet. Only trouble is, he's Mexican. If you don't like enchiladas, tortillas, chili burros, well . . ."

In the dining room, they found Lieftin and Abdu sitting at the same table. Both men were picking at their food and looking very disgruntled. Carmody invited himself to sit with them, and Gilson followed his example. Gilson was introduced as a businessman.

"Has your request for an interview with Yess been denied?" Carmody asked Lieftin.

Lieftin growled and said, "They were polite but they made it clear that I couldn't see him until after the Night."

"You could take the Sleep," Carmody said, then paused. "Hmm, if Yess forbids Sleep, will he make the edict apply to non-Kareenans, too?"

"Do you mean that I could Sleep and then interview Yess afterwards?" Lieftin said, his face red. "Nothing doing!"

Carmody wondered why Lieftin was so vehement. If Lieftin were the assassin, he would want to complete his job before the Night started.

"Are you going back now?" Carmody said to Abdu. "You can't complete any business now."

"This restriction handicaps me," Abdu answered, "but I can conduct business over the phone."

"I wouldn't think you could do much during the festival. Most businesses are shut down now."

"Kareenans are like Terrestrials. There are always a few who'll do business no matter what, even during an earthquake."

Lieftin jerked a thumb toward the entrance to the hotel. "See those two guys dressed in the blue and red feathers? They're cops. They're making sure we don't leave this forsaken tomb."

"It is quiet," Carmody said. He looked around. Aside from a waiter standing ten tables away, they were the only ones in the dining room. Moreover, the lobby beyond was occupied only by several desk clerks and bellhops, all silent and glum.

"I can't stand my room," Lieftin said. "It's like being in a mausoleum. All that cold stone and deathly silence. How the, uh, how do the Kareenans stand living in places like this?"

"They have certain resemblances to the ancient Egyptians," the bishop said. "They think much of death and their short stay on this planet. They like to be reminded that this is only a stopping-off place."

"What's their idea of Heaven? And hell?" Abdu said.

Carmody started to speak, then waited for Lieftin to answer. If Lieftin really were what he claimed to be, he would

112

have to know at least the elements of Kareenan religion. His church was not likely to send an unbriefed man here on such a mission; spaceship travel cost too much.

Lieftin started to eat, his eyes on his plate. When it became evident he was not going to reply to Abdu, Carmody said, "Boontism has a two-level Heaven. The bottom level is for those who are worshipers of Yess, who strive to be 'good' but do not dare to test themselves by going through the Night. These live forever in a place similar to their earthly existence. That is, they must work, sleep, they have discomforts, pain, frustration, boredom, etc. But they do live forever.

"The top level is for those worshipers of Yess who successfully dare the Night. These are supposed to enjoy eternal ecstasy, a mystical ecstasy. The experience, you might say, is like that which the saved of the Christian religion. They see God face to face, only in this case it's the mystical face of Yess, the glory behind the fleshly mask of Yess. No one sees Boonta, not even Her son."

"What about their Hell?" Abdu said.

"There are two Hells, also. The lower level is for the religiously indifferent, the lukewarms, the hypocrites, the self-deceived. And also for those who dared the Night but failed. You see, that's one of the reasons why so few Yessites stay Awake. It's true that the rewards of success are worth the ordeal. But failure casts you down into Hell. And there are always so many failures. It's safer not to take a chance and so go to Heaven's lower level.

"The top layer of Hell is reserved for the true Algulists. And these have their own ecstasy, analogous to that which the high-level Yessites enjoy. Only it's a dark joy, the orgasm of evil. Inferior to that of Heaven's, but, if you're a genuine Algulist, you prefer it. Evil craves evil, wants nothing but evil."

"It's a crazy religion," Lieftin said.

"The Kareenans say the same thing about ours."

Carmody excused himself, leaving Gilson to his own devices, and went back to his room. He had Gilson called to the phone.

"I'm going out for a while. I want to see an old friend of mine, a Kareenan. And I also want to give Fratt a chance to strike. Maybe that way I can get hold of him, either neutralize him or talk him into some sense. Certainly I can find out then who he is and what I did that makes him so bent on revenge."

"He might get you first."

"I'm well aware of that. Oh, another thing. I'm going to call Tand and see if he can use his influence again. I want him to release you from restriction. Not for the Fratt case. You should watch our prime suspect, Lieftin. If he makes a break, as I strongly believe he will, I don't want you hampered in trailing him."

"Thanks," Gilson said. "I'll keep an eye on him."

Carmody cut the operative off, and he spoke Tand's number to the receiver. Tand's face appeared on the screen.

"You're lucky," he said. "I was just leaving. What can I do for you?"

Carmody told him what he wanted. Tand replied that there would be no difficulty. He would put the order through immediately.

"Actually, we can use extra help. We don't have anybody to shadow Lieftin if he does get loose, as he can, if he's ingenious enough."

"The old Lieftin could do it," the priest said.

"I'll tell you the truth. It's not only Earth assassins we're worried about. The Algulists will be making their moves before the Night begins. When I say Algulist, I'm not only talking about those who've gotten through the Night. I'm talking about the entire secret society, which is largely composed of those who have not chanced the Night. Our government is honeycombed with them, and I say this knowing that our conversation may be monitored."

"There's something I don't understand," Carmody said. "Why are those Algulists who passed the Night during the reign of Yess still living? You remember when I'd been caught by the statue and had not made up my mind which way I was going, whether I'd choose the six of Yess or the six of Algul? Well, when I did make my choice, and it was definitely ascertained that Mary's baby would be Yess, the would-be Fathers of Algul tried to run away. But they died.

"Now, I had always thought that Algulists survived the Night only if Algul won. Yet I've heard from you and others that successfully beNighted Algulists survive, are living right now. Why?"

"Those you saw die did so because we six Fathers, consciously, and you unconsciously, willed them to die. But there were other Algulists, not Fathers, who survived. They did not die because we did not know about them.

"It's illegal to be an Algulist, you know. The penalty is death. Of course, if Algul should ever win—Boonta forbid

—then you may be sure that any Yessite who's caught will be executed. And much more painfully than an Algulist now dies."

"Thank you, Tand. I'm going now to visit Mrs. Kri. I presume she's still living at the old place?"

"I really couldn't say. I haven't seen or heard of her for many years."

Carmody ordered a costume sent up to him, one with a large mask, that of a trogur bird. He put it on and then left the hotel, after having presented his credentials to the guards stationed at the main doorway. Before leaving, he looked into the dining room and saw that Gilson, Lieftin, and Abdu had left. However, about a dozen non-Kareenans were dining. They, too, looked depressed.

Outside, the tomb-like silence of the hotel gave way to a storm of music, shouts, screams, tootling of horns, whistles, firecrackers, drums, and bull-roarers. The streets were jammed with a noisy chaos of costume-clad merrymakers.

Carmody slowly made his much-jostled way through the mob. After about fifteen minutes, he managed to get to a side street which was much less populated. He walked for another fifteen minutes before he saw a taxi. The cabbie was not very eager to take a fare, but Carmody insisted. Grumbling beneath his breath, the driver eased the car through the crowds, and presently they were in a district through which they could drive with reasonable speed. Even so, the taxi had to stop now and then to nudge through clots of masquers walking toward the main streets.

It was a half-hour before the taxi halted in front of Mrs. Kri's house. By then, the huge moon of Kareen was up, shedding its silver confetti on the black and gray stones of the massive houses. Carmody got out, paid the driver, and asked him to wait. The driver, who apparently resigned himself to missing the fun, agreed.

Carmody strode up the walk, then stopped to look at the tree that had once been Mr. Kri. It had grown much larger since he had last seen it. It towered at least thirty-five meters high, and its branches spread out across the yard.

"Hello, Mr. Kri," the priest said.

He went on by the unresponding man-plant to clang the huge knocker on the big iron door. There were no lights in the windows, and he began to wonder if he had been too hasty. He should have phoned first. But Mrs. Kri would be old by now, since the geriatrics of Earth was available only to wealthy Kareenans. He had taken it for granted that she would be staying home.

He clanged the knocker again. Silence. He turned to walk away, and as he did so he heard the door creak open behind him. A voice called, "Who is it?"

Carmody returned, taking off his mask.

"John Carmody, Earthman," he said. Light streamed out of the doorway. In it stood an old female. But it was not Mrs. Kri.

"I lived here at one time," he said. "Long ago. I thought I'd drop by to see Mrs. Kri."

The shriveled-up old woman seemed frightened at confronting an alien from interstellar space. She closed the door until only part of her face showed, and said in a quavering voice, "Mrs. Kri doesn't live here any more."

"Would you mind telling me where I might find her?" Carmody asked gently.

"I don't know. She decided to go through the last Night, and that's the last anyone ever heard of her."

"I'm sorry to hear that," Carmody said, and meant it. Despite her testiness and flightiness, he had been fond of Mrs. Kri.

He returned to the taxi. As he drew near, the headbeams of another car swung around the nearby corner, and a car sped toward him. Carmody dived under the taxi, thinking as he did so that he was probably making a fool of himself. But he did not usually argue with his hunches.

Nor was he wrong this time. Gunfire exploded; glass shattered. The taxi driver screamed. Then the car was gone down the street, gathering speed as it went. Its tires screeched going around a corner, and it disappeared.

Carmody started to rise. Something flashed just before his head came above the window of the car. He was hurled backward, blinded and deafened.

When he managed to get to his feet again, he was enveloped in bitter smoke. Fire spurted upward from the interior of the car and revealed, through the blown-open door on his side, the body half-hanging out of the car.

He ran back to the house and beat the knocker repeatedly against the tightly shut door. There was no sound within. He did not blame the old woman for not answering him; probably she was calling the police.

He picked up his mask, replaced it over his head, and started walking. The ringing went out of his ears and the dazzle out of his eyes. In two minutes he was inside a public phone booth. He called Gilson at the hotel, but the operative did not answer. He tried Lieftin. This time, a Kareenan policeman appeared on the screen.

At the policeman's request, Carmody took his mask off. The Kareenan's eyes widened on seeing the Earth Father of Yess, and his manner became very respectful.

"The Terrestrial, Lieftin, escaped over an hour ago," he said. "Apparently, he used some sort of thermit to melt the bars over the windows and lowered himself by a rope he must have had in his luggage. We have an all-points out for him, but he is in a costume. He had it delivered by a bellhop."

"Check on the Terrestrial, Raphael Abdu, for me, will you?" Carmody said. "Do you know where Gilson is?"

"Gilson left shortly after Lieftin escaped. Wait. We'll check on Abdu for the Father."

Carmody's watch indicated five minutes passed before the officer's face appeared again. He said, "The Terrestrial Abdu is in his room, Father."

His face disappeared, but his voice said, "Just a moment."

Apparently, he was talking to somebody else. "All right," the policeman muttered. His face came back. "Gilson just sent in a message for you. You're to call him at this number."

Carmody spoke the number given him into the receiver. Gilson's face came into view. Loud voices and laughter came through the receiver.

"I'm in a tavern on Wiilgrar and Tuwdon Streets," Gilson said. "Just a minute while I put my mask back on. I took it off so you'd be sure it was me."

"What's up?" Carmody said. "By the way, I know about Lieftin's escape."

"You do? Well, I tailed him. He's in the tavern here, talking with another fellow. A Kareenan, I'm sure. I got a good look at his fingernails and the back of his neck. Lieftin is dressed in a brown costume that's supposed to represent some sort of animal. The Kareenan equivalent of a deer, I guess. His mask is an animal face with antlers. His buddy is dressed in a catlike outfit."

Probably Ardour and Eeshquur, Carmody thought. He knew enough about the prominent figures of Kareenan mythology and fairy tale to identify them. But he did not take time to acquaint Gilson with his knowledge.

"Can you stick around there until I get a taxi? I'll tell you what happened to me later."

117

He cut Gilson off and phoned for a taxi. It was ten minutes before one showed up. However, stimulated by the large sum of money Carmody offered, the driver broke every traffic law as the opportunity offered itself. Carmody could not complain that the trip took longer than it should.

Tiiwit's Tavern was well off the main street of the city of Rak, but it was crowded tonight. The festive mobs had spilled out this way after the parade had broken up. Gilson, costumed in the trogur dress similar to the priest's, was waiting outside. Carmody talked with him for a minute, then followed him in.

Lieftin and the Kareenan were sitting at a table in the shadowy rear. The Kareenan was gesticulating in a manner that reminded Carmody of someone he had met recently. When the Kareenan got up and went to the washroom, his walk identified him.

"It's Abog," Carmody said to Gilson, "Rilg's secretary. Now, what in hell is he doing here talking with Lieftin?"

Abog would not be doing this on his own, just for pleasure. Was his boss, Rilg, a member of the Algulist underground? He could have heard of the assassin sent by the Earth fanatics and decided to use him for his own purposes.

"Listen, Gilson," Carmody said, "we'd better be careful from now on when we're dealing with the police. Some of them may be working for Rilg. You get out of here and go back to the hotel. If I'm picked up, I stand a better chance of careful treatment. I'll stick close to Lieftin."

Gilson said, "I hate to let you do it."

"I know this world better than you. Besides, unless you're planning to Night, you won't be here much longer."

The operative left, wishing Carmody good luck. The priest stood by the bar for a while, sipping Kareenan beer. When a couple rose from a table near Lieftin's and staggered out, Carmody seated himself. So noisy was the tavern, he could not hear what Lieftin and Abog were saying. It was unfortunate that he had not taken a tapper with him. With it, he could have beamed in on the two and eavesdropped.

Abruptly, the two rose and walked swiftly toward the door. Carmody waited a moment before following. Evidently they were on the alert, for Abog kept glancing behind him. The two went out the door when Carmody was halfway across the room.

A moment later, three policemen appeared in the doorway, blocking it. Carmody stopped and looked back. More policemen were coming through the back door.

Could Abog and Lieftin have spotted him or Gilson?

Carmody did not believe it. More likely, they were just taking precautions—making sure that anyone trying to follow them would be held up by the police.

Carmody angled off, staggering, toward the washroom. He went through the door just as whistles shrilled and the alarmed patrons began to shout. Unobserved, he went through the open window of the washroom.

As he dropped like a cat onto the paved alley, a voice said, "Hold it! Hands above the head!"

Lifting his hands, Carmody turned. He saw a policeman standing there with a gun pointed at him.

"Turn back around! Hands on the wall! Quick!"

"I ain't doing nothing, officer!" Carmody whined in lower-class Kareenan. He started to obey, then lifted his mask, flipped it at the policeman's face and continued his turn, violently. The policeman said, "Ugh!" The gun fired, and the bullet exploded against the stone wall. Flying stone chips struck Carmody. He rolled into the officer's legs, knocked him over forward. Before the officer could get up, he found Carmody astride his back. Then he went limp as the priest pressed with his thumbs on the areas just behind the ears.

Carmody picked up the gun and mask. As he ran toward the far end of the alley, he put the mask on and stuck the gun in his belt. There were whistles behind him, then shouts. As Carmody threw himself forward on the ground, bullets shattered chips off the wall ahead of him. He kept on rolling around the corner, was up on his feet and running again. Within a minute, he was back in the street and mingling with the crowd. A police car drove slowly through the mob, its siren hooting. Carmody stood by and watched it go.

There was not much for him to do now; he had lost Abog and Lieftin. He might as well go back to the hotel.

From the hotel lobby, he phoned Gilson's room. There was no reply. He called Tand and was told by a servant that Tand was not expected back until early in the morning. Carmody went up to his floor with two policemen, unlocked the door, and asked them to search his suite. They reported that it was empty of intruders and seemed to contain no suspicious devices. He thanked them and bolted the door after them.

After drinking a cup of wine, Carmody made up his bed to look as if someone were sleeping under the covers. He spread a blanket under a table and, concealed by the heavy tablecloth, curled up and went to sleep.

He awoke with the phone ringing on the table above him.

Instead of rolling out and springing up to the phone, he peered from beneath the tablecloth. The morning light was filtering through the iron bars and the double glass of the windows. All looked safe, so he crawled out from under the table. His muscles were stiff and sore from the exertions of the night before and his cramped position.

Tand was calling. He looked as if he had slept even less well than Carmody. His face was drawn, and there were harsh lines raying out from the corners of his nostrils down to the edges of his lips. Nevertheless, he smiled.

"Did you enjoy your first night's stay at our hotel?"

"It wasn't boring," Carmody replied. He looked at the clock on the wall. "Almost lunch time. I slept through breakfast."

"I have good news," Tand said. "Yess will see you tonight. At the hour of the thrugu."

"Very good. Now, tell me, do you think there's a chance our line is being tapped?"

"Who knows? It could be. Why?"

"I'd like to talk to you. Right now. It's very important."

"I haven't slept all night," Tand said. "But then who does at this time? All right. Why don't you come to my place? Or would you prefer another place?"

"Your house could be bugged."

Tand lost his smile. "It's that bad? Very well. I'll drive myself, pick you up in front of the hotel. I'll be there in half an hour."

While waiting in his room, Carmody walked back and forth, his arms swinging violently up and down as if he were striding across fields on a hike. The name Fratt beat like a gavel. Fratt! Fratt! Who was Fratt? Where? When? Why?

He had an excellent memory, undimmed and unblocked. He remembered well the hideous crimes he had committed. There had been a time when he had thought the only way he would be able to stop remembering them would be to kill himself. That was long ago. Now, he could visualize all he had done, but it was as if he were looking at someone else.

But why could he not summon the man Fratt from the past?

He ran through the names of all the victims he could recollect. There were many. Then he tried to visualize the anonymous faces, of which there were also many.

By the time he had to leave his room, he had given up. He also had a slight headache, something he had not suffered for many years. Was it caused by his conscience? Was there still something lurking in his unconscious, when he thought he had cleansed himself of guilt and remorse?

He walked out of the hotel door just as Tand drove up in a long sleek black car. Its right door opened before Carmody got to it, and it closed after Carmody settled himself beside Tand in the front seat.

"This is a Ghruzha," Tand said with some pride. "It is modeled after the Earth GM Stego, you'll notice."

Tand left the main street and drove to a residential district. He stopped the car by a children's playground. "Don't worry about tappers beaming in on us," he said. "I have a scrambler working."

Carmody told his friend of the previous night's happenings.

Tand said, "I've suspected something of the sort. But there's nothing we can do. We don't have any concrete evidence on which to act. Now, we could confront Abog with your accusations, but what could we do with them? In the first place, you don't really know whether or not the man in the Eeshquur costume was Abog. You may be sure, but you can't, in the legal sense, positively identify him. Moreover, say you could. So he was talking to an Earthman in a tavern. Is that anything unusual during the pre-Night festival? And he could claim he didn't even know that Lieftin was an Earthman."

"No, he couldn't," Carmody said. "I doubt that Lieftin can speak Kareenan like a native."

"You can't prove anything," Tand said in English. "However, as you Terrestrials say, forewarned is four-armed."

Carmody laughed, for he appreciated the pun. Tand had made the sign that Kareenan children and superstitious rurals used to ward off the evil spirit Duublow, who is supposed to have four arms with which he catches unwary travelers at crossroads before devouring them.

Tand continued, "Rilg may not be an Algulist at all. He may think of himself as a very devout Yessite. But he is chief of our overgovernment, and his first concern will be the survival of the state and the welfare of Kareen. I don't envy his position. He'll be torn between his religious inclination to accept whatever his god says and his desire to preserve the status quo. Plus his doubts about his own ability to survive the Night. The last element is, I would say, the strongest in him, as it will be in most people.

"However, what he can't see, as the majority can't see, is

121

that a purge has to be faced up to at some time. So why not now, no matter how painful? Believe me, the very resistance that so many have expressed illustrates how shallow the faith of most is. It's easy to follow the most popular religion, to worship the victorious god. But when you're called on to make the supreme test, that's different."

"Yess is separating the men from the boys?"

"That's a good way to put it."

"But the children!"

Tand grimaced. "I don't relish the idea. But the whole idea would be defeated if they were not subjected to the Night."

"That's not logical," the priest said. "Suppose the Night does leave none but the good to breed? What about their children? You can't say that goodness—whatever that is by your definition—is a genetic trait."

"No, but children tend, generally, to be what their parents are. In any case, it won't matter. Because, once Yess decrees a general Waking, there will be no more Sleeping. All will go through every Night."

"All right, I can see there's no use arguing about this particular point. So, what are you going to do about Rilg and Abog?"

"Enforce the precautions taken to guard Yess. And to guard you. I've already had your belongings moved to a room on the fourteenth floor. The men who were guarding you will be replaced by men I know I can trust. You won't take a step outside your room without adequate protection."

Carmody said, "That seems reasonable, if restricting. Oh, by the way, could you make provisions for the widow and orphans of the poor taxi driver? I'm not really responsible for his death, but, if it hadn't been for me, he'd still be alive."

"I've already done that," Tand replied. He smiled grimly. "However, the money may not do them much good. It depends on how they get through the Night. And whether or not money is worth anything afterward."

Tand started the car and drove back toward the hotel. Carmody was silent for a long time. His cardinal had given him instructions to try to persuade Yess from forcing a universal Waking. But it looked as if that might be just the thing to desire, from the Church viewpoint. If Kareenan civilization collapsed, the Kareenans would not be doing any extensive missionary work for a long time.

From the humane point of view, however, the cardinal was correct. But Carmody doubted that the cardinal and his superior had even considered this. To them, removed a million and a half light-years from an alien culture, the results of Yess' decision would not be apparent. They would be thinking only of what a thoroughly Yessed and doubtless zealous people would do. They were visualizing swarms of fanatics descending upon Earth and the colonial planets.

What should he urge upon Yess? That, contrary to the cardinal's instructions, he should encourage the decision for all to pass through the Night? Or should he follow his orders and act contrary to the interests of the Church, even if the Church did not know it?

There was no doubt in Carmody's mind. Prevent the slaughter and the pain and misery. He could not be a Christian and do otherwise. His superiors would have to understand that only a man on the spot was capable of knowing the situation well. And that such a man, if he were a *man*, would disobey. Should his superiors not sympathize, then they would have to punish him as they thought fit. He was ready.

He had only one doubt. What if things were not going to be as bad as Tand and so many others thought? Yess, a being superior to ordinary mortals, might know much more than they.

Tand let him off at the hotel entrance. Three Kareenans in civilian clothes hastened to the car to escort Carmody. Tand said, "I'll send a car around to pick you up tonight. I'll meet you outside Yess' quarters in the Temple and brief you before you have your audience."

Carmody thanked him and returned to his room, now on the fourteenth floor. Tand's men stationed themselves in the hallway. He phoned Gilson's room but got no reply. He called the desk clerk and asked if Gilson had left any message for him. The clerk replied that Mr. Gilson had not checked in since he left last night.

Carmody was worried. After making several calls and being unable to get into touch with Tand, he asked to speak to the largh, the lieutenant, in charge of the police who had previously guarded him. These had been ordered to other duties. But a largh had been detailed to continue the investigation.

Largh Piinal was in the lobby. He came up immediately, however, to talk to Carmody in his room. Piinal was a young Kareenan, very tall, thin, and solemn.

"You suspect foul play?" he said.

"There's a chance of it," Carmody said. He had not told Piinal all about the previous night's incident. His story was that Gilson had located Lieftin at Tiiwit's tavern. Carmody had come after being phoned and had watched Lieftin for a while. He did not mention his suspicions about Abog. Gilson had then followed Lieftin from the tavern, but Carmody had been unable to go with him. He had been due at the hotel to answer a call from Tand. He did not mention the incident with the policeman in the alley, either.

"I can try to put some men on the case," Piinal said. "But you must understand that the festival strains our capacities. Also, that the streets are filled with masked people the clock around. People dance and drink and make love until they drop, then sleep a few hours and continue. So, it will be very difficult to identify anybody, even an Earthman."

"I understand," the priest replied. "I think I should make the search myself. I might recognize Gilson's walk and gestures even when he has a mask on."

"I have orders to secure your safety," the largh said. "I can't do that if you're out in the crowd. I'm sorry, Father, but that's the way it has to be."

"The Father Tand has given me three men to watch over me," Carmody said.

"I apologize, Father, but you can't go out now. Father Tand's men can guard you, but I have authority over them."

The phone rang. Piinal, closer to it, answered. A policeman's face appeared. He said, "Windru reporting, sir. It's about the Earthman, Gilson. He's been found; he's dead. In an alley near the Thrudhu Block. About ten minutes ago. Stabbed twice in the back and his throat cut."

Carmody groaned, and he said, "Windru, has positive identification been made?"

Windru looked at his superior, and the largh said, "It's all right. Speak."

"Yes, Father. His papers were in his beltbag. His prints and photo checked."

Piinal excused himself, saying that he had to make arrangements to deliver the body. Apparently, the ETS had an agreement with the Kareenan authorities to ship any of their dead agents back to Earth for burial. Carmody thought that Piinal was eager to use this as an excuse to keep from talking to him.

Angry, he put in another call to Tand, only to be told that he could not be reached. He began pacing back and forth across the room. It was very frustrating to have to remain closeted up; he wanted to do something.

He was certain that Lieftin was connected with Gilson's death. Probably Abog was also guilty. But he could do nothing

124

about it, nothing. And where was Lieftin? Wherever he was, he was working toward the accomplishment of his task: the murder of Yess.

Carmody became furious enough to curse the group of Earthmen, his own religionists, who had hired Lieftin. How strange that the disciples of Algul and the disciples of Christ had banded together!

The door-knocker clanged, muffled by the thick iron. Carmody shot the bolt and pushed one side of the door to let it swing out and so notify the policemen that they could enter. The door continued swinging, and two Kareenans stepped through. They had guns in their hands. Behind them, out in the hall, were two other males. They were beginning to drag in the bodies of the guards.

Carmody, his arms raised, backed up. While one man held a gun on him, the other went back into the hall to help the rest bring in the policemen. These were not dead, as Carmody had first thought. They were unconscious, sleeping as if drugged.

A Kareenan handed the priest a costume and mask. "Put them on." Carmody obeyed. "Are you working for Fratt?" he asked, but none of the five answered him.

After he had dressed himself and put on the mask, an antlered Ardour head, he was told to come with the others. They would be behind him. If he tried to run or call for help, he would be shot in the leg.

The Kareenans, also masked now, looking like any other group of merry-makers, took him to the end of the hall. There, they told him to walk up the steps. At the fifteenth floor, he was taken back down the hall to a room exactly above his. One of the group beat the knocker twice rapidly, and after a five-second pause, three times.

The door swung open, and a gun was stuck in Carmody's back. There was nothing he could do but enter. He had not seen another guest or hotel employee in either hall.

The door was closed behind him, and the bolt shot home with a thud. The mask taken from his face, he could examine the room. It was furnished like his; the doors to the two other rooms of the suite were open.

By the stone table in the middle of the room stood Raphael Abdu. An aged Earthwoman sat beside the table. She wore clothes which had been in style thirty years ago, but there were certain features about them that had a colonial look. Carmody could not place their origin. The woman had long white hair plaited and coiled into a huge pile on top of

125

her head. Her wrinkled face looked as if it had once been beautiful. Her eyes were concealed behind large hexagonal sunglasses.

"Are you absolutely sure it's John Carmody?" she said to Abdu in non-Terrestrial English.

Impatiently, Abdu said, "Don't be ridiculous! Do you want him to speak so you can recognize his voice?"

"Yes!"

"Speak up, Carmody," Abdu growled. "Give us a few phrases from some of your sermons. The lady wants to hear you."

"Ah, Fratt. I made a natural mistake," Carmody said. "I assumed that you were a man. Obviously, you had a man dictate the letter for you."

"That's him!" she cried. "I haven't forgotten that voice! Even after all these years!"

She placed a thick-veined hand on Abdu's.

"Pay the others off. Tell them to get lost."

"Glad to," Abdu said. He went into the room on Carmody's right and returned immediately with a large bundle of Kareenan paper currency. He counted out each man's share and waited while they checked the amount. Four left the suite, but one stayed behind. He stripped Carmody and taped his arms behind him. He sat Carmody down in one of the huge chairs and taped his ankles together. A rope from underneath his cloak was then used to bind the priest's waist to the chair. Two more strips of tape went over Carmody's shoulders and under his armpits to secure him to the back of the chair.

"His mouth?" the Kareenan said. Abdu translated into English for her.

"No," the woman replied. "I can always shut him up if I want to. Just leave the tape on the table here."

"I still don't know who you are," Carmody said.

"Your memory is too clogged with evil deeds," she said. "But I haven't forgotten. That's the important thing."

The Kareenan went through the door, and Abdu bolted it after him. There was silence for a while. Carmody studied her features. Suddenly, memory came swimming up from within.

She was the woman from whom he had gotten the layout of the fortress in which the Staronif Shootfire jewel was guarded.

He had gone to the colonial planet of Beulah to hide. Raspold and others had been hot on his trail on Springboard, but he had escaped. On Beulah, a planet settled largely by Englishmen and Scandinavians, he had played the part of a prospector. He had ignored the challenge of the Staronif jewel for a long time because he had been determined to stay out of trouble.

But when it looked as if Raspold had lost him, he established his assumed identity; he could no longer resist the temptation. His careful planning took four months, really not much time when the size of the job was considered. He had gathered a number of criminals, Lieftin among them. After assuring an escape by spaceship from Beulah, he had bribed one of the guards of the Staronif jewel, a considerable feat in itself; the guards were famous for their honesty. The guard was to open the doors for them, after having silenced the alarm mechanism. He had given them a plan of the rooms and of the warning devices installed in the vault where the Staronif was put at night.

But the demo who ruled one of the small states of Beulah had decided that things were too stagnant. He had discharged all the guards, hired new ones, and begun making alterations in the protective mechanisms and even in the internal construction of the building. Carmody had been afraid that the guard might start talking if he thought his usefulness was over and he would be cut out of his share. He had to be killed, and Carmody killed him.

The others in his group had wanted to give up the robbery, but Carmody had insisted they continue. Moreover, they were to stick to the schedule. After some investigation, he found that the demo's secretary had not been discharged or transferred to another job. The rumor was that she was also the demo's mistress; he could not bear to give her up. Carmody had entered the woman's house the night before the robbery was to take place.

Mrs. Geraldine Fratt, as she called herself, was with a man—her son. He lived in another state and happened to be visiting his mother. When the mother proved resistant even to Carmody's tortures, and when it looked as if she would die before revealing anything, he began to work on the son. She could not stand watching her son being cut apart, even though he had begged her not to talk because of him.

Mrs. Fratt had led the way into the fortress. Her son was carried along by Lieftin and another man to make sure that she did not betray them. After the Staronif had been removed from its vault, Carmody had shoved the mother and son into it. Then he had tossed in a grenade and closed the vault door.

It was the explosion that had set off an alarm and had forced Carmody and his men to run, instead of making the planned leisurely drive to the spaceship. Raspold, having just arrived on Beulah in his search, had joined the chase.

During the flight, Carmody stole a gravplane. Forced down near the edge of the Big Thorn Forest, he had gone on foot. And it was in that forest that he had been compelled to shove the Staronif down the throat of the lugar. Later, he had made his escape from Beulah and eventually had gone to Dante's Joy.

"I think I overlooked you, Mrs. Fratt," he said, "because, one, I thought a man had sent me that letter and, two, I thought that you and your son were dead."

"My son protected me with his own body," she said. "He died. My face was mangled, and my eyes were destroyed by flying fragments. I had my face repaired, but these . . ."

She removed her glasses, and Carmody could see the empty sockets.

"But you could have had new eyes!" he said.

"I swore I would never see again until you were paid back for what you did to me and Bart. I've spent a lot of time and money looking for you. I had a great deal of money, you know, because the demo willed me a fortune when he died. But it was almost all gone when I finally heard about your being a priest on Wildenwooly. By that time, I'd quit buying jerries because I wanted to reserve all my money for the search. That's why I'm so old-looking now. I was afraid I'd die before you were found. But, thank God, I did find you."

"You've taken all these years to find me?" he said. "Mrs. Fratt, what kind of men did you hire to look for me?"

"Raphael Abdu conducted the search for me. Don't you say anything against him, you evil-tongued monster! He's a good and faithful man; he's been working tirelessly for me too long. I know him and trust him."

"So that now, when he's bled you of your money and there's no more coming, he conveniently discovers me?" the priest said. "Well, give him credit for that. At least, he didn't just drop the whole thing. He did give you something for keeping him in what I imagine was a good-paying job for twenty-eight or twenty-nine years. Ah, thou good and faithful servant!"

"Should I shut his mouth, Mrs. Fratt?" Abdu said. "I could knock his teeth out. It'd be a good starter."

"No, let him talk. I don't care what he says; he can't change my mind."

"Mrs. Fratt, Abdu could have found me easily any time after I left this planet. I was in Johns Hopkins for a year. The police knew where I was, and my Church had no reason to hide my identity or location. Abdu's taken you for a sucker."

"You're a slippery one," she said. "You escaped the first man Abdu sent after you, and you've made it difficult for us to catch you. But you're here now, and nothing anyone can do is going to get you out of this."

Carmody, despite the mausoleum coolness of the room, was sweating.

"Mrs. Fratt," he said without any inflection of the desperation he felt, "I can understand why you want revenge on me. I partly understand, anyway, although after all these years and the fact that I am no longer the man you knew . . . Still, I cannot understand or forgive you for having murdered an innocent woman, my wife!"

She clutched the arms of the chair. "What? What are you talking about?"

"You know damn well what I'm talking about!" he said harshly. "You had my Anna murdered! And when you did that, you became as guilty and as foul as that John Carmody you hate so much. You are as wicked as he was, and you have no right to talk of justice or retribution!"

"What do you mean?" she shrilled, turning her blind head toward Abdu and then back to Carmody. "What's this about your wife? I didn't even know you had a wife! Murdered, you say? Murdered?"

Abdu spoke smoothly and even managed a chuckle of amusement, but he glared at Carmody. "I told you you have to be careful of him, Mrs. Fratt. He's slick as Satan himself. He's just saying that about his wife to throw you off the track, to confuse you. And to implant suspicions about me in your mind. His wife's all right. I saw her kiss him goodby just before he left Wildenwooly."

Mrs. Fratt's expression was angry. "You liar, Carmody! Would you say anything to save your own skin?"

"I am telling the truth!" Carmody said. "My wife was killed by a bomb. And shortly after she died, I got a phone call from a man wearing a mask. He said that you were responsible for Anna's murder!"

"You lie!"

"Then perhaps you can explain another thing. If you wanted me alive, why did your men try to kill me outside the house of an old friend of mine, here in Rak?"

She became even paler; her mouth worked soundlessly.

"In your hatred for me, you not only had my wife killed, you caused the death of an innocent man, one who had nothing to do with me except that he happened to drive the taxi that took me out to Mrs. Kri's. He was killed by the bomb meant for me."

"He's lying again," Abdu shouted savagely. "He'll say anything to put off the inevitable, the justified inevitable, I'll swear."

Mrs. Fratt reached out, touched Abdu, slid her hand along him, and gripped his hand. "You didn't do all these terrible things, did you? You didn't kill his wife and that man, did you? Or try to kill Carmody and rob me of him?"

"I'm telling you the truth, Mrs. Fratt. I think you'd better quit listening to him. He could talk a hungry snake away from a bird."

He looked at his watch. "Mrs. Fratt, we've ten hours before the last ship leaves. We'd better get started. You didn't want this to be a short thing, remember?"

"Oh, I made a mistake not getting eyes before I did this!" she said. "I want to see him suffer! But there wasn't time to do it!"

"Never mind, you can hear him. And feel him."

"Mrs. Fratt," Carmody said, unable to keep his voice from going hoarse, "I'm making one last appeal. You spoke of God a little while ago, thanked Him. Do you really believe that He'll approve this? If you are a Christian, then for the sake of God don't do this! Even if I were the man who wronged you so, He would not want you to torture me. *Revenge is mine, saith the Lord*. But I am not . . ."

"*Revenge is mine, saith the Lord!*" Mrs. Fratt almost hissed. "The Devil may quote scripture, and I guess that is true! But go ahead! Whine, beg, plead for mercy! I begged, for my son's sake, and you laughed at me! Laugh now!"

Carmody fell silent. He was determined that he would at least try to die with dignity. They would get no pleas or screams of pain until he could stand it no longer. Nevertheless, he could not control the quivering of his body.

He said, "Mrs. Fratt, while I can talk and think rationally, I want to tell you that I forgive you. I hope you have a chance for God to forgive you, too. So, no matter what I say later, remember that this is my true feeling. God grant you grace."

Mrs. Fratt had risen to her feet. She started to walk slowly toward him, with Abdu holding her hand. She stopped and put her hand to her heart. She was silent so until Abdu said, "It's just another trick, Mrs. Fratt."

"Help me, Raphael," Mrs. Fratt said in a low voice. "Help me."

"I'll be your strength," Abdu said. He went to the table and lifted the cloth aside. Steel glittered under the light. Long sharp knives, surgeon's scalpels, a surgical bit and drill, a saw. There were also splinters of the Kareenan duurl, a bamboolike, wood; a rubber syringe with a long, slightly curved beak; several wires; a pair of scissors; a pair of pliers with broad thin edges; a club, and a hammer.

Abdu picked up a scalpel, walked to Mrs. Fratt, placed the scalpel in her hand.

"I think he ought at least to have his face marked up a little bit. He ought to feel something of the pain you felt, Mrs. Fratt."

She touched the scalpel gingerly, then drew her hand back.

"If you get faint-hearted now, Mrs. Fratt, you'll have wasted all those years. Have you gone blind for nothing?"

She shook her head. "Let me feel his face. I can't see, but maybe if I can see it through my fingers, I can hate as much as I did when I first saw it. God! I never thought I'd shrink from this! I used to cry because I couldn't have him in my power."

She walked close to Carmody. Her right hand went out, touched his forehead. It jumped back, then returned, moved over his features.

He closed his teeth on her hand. She cried out and tried to jerk back her hand, but his jaws held her. He brought his feet up; though taped at the ankles, they had not been tied to the chair. They came up together between her legs and in a spasm of power he lifted her a few inches. She cried out again at the blow. Abdu yelled and started to run up to help her.

Carmody pulled his legs up against his chest in a contortion that cost him pain. His mouth opened; the woman jerked her hand loose and staggered back. His legs straightened; his feet caught her in the pit of the stomach. Doubling over, she reeled against Abdu. Then she straightened and fell to the floor.

Abdu stared at the bloody scalpel in his hand and at the

blood spurting from her back. He dropped the knife and went down on one knee beside Mrs. Fratt.

He called to her vainly, listened to her heart, and finally rose.

"The scalpel didn't go in deep enough to kill her. You killed her when you kicked her, you bastard!"

"I didn't want to," Carmody gasped. "I wouldn't have had to except for you. But I was damned if I'd just sit here and let her cut me up."

"You're damned anyway," Abdu said slowly. "That trick won't work twice."

He picked up the scalpel and moved to one side of Carmody.

"What's your interest, Abdu? You've made a good living from her. Isn't that enough? Why should you want to torture me?"

"Sure, I led her on, and I lived like a king. But I was fond of the old lady, even if she was a sucker. Besides, I always wanted to see what kind of stuff you're made of."

Behind the chair now, he crooked his left arm around Carmody's head to hold it steady. The scalpel nicked into Carmody's cheek and cut downward.

"Does that hurt, Carmody?" Abdu said in the priest's ear.

"Enough," Carmody whispered.

"Let's see how tender the skin of your lips is."

The scalpel slashed the corner of his mouth. Carmody went rigid, but clamped his teeth together to keep from crying out.

Abdu placed the blade against Carmody's jugular vein. "One slash and it'd be all over. How'd you like that?"

"I'm afraid I'd like it very much," Carmody said. "God forgive me."

"Yeah, it'd be a kind of suicide, wouldn't it? Well, if there is a Hell, I hope you go to it. But don't get eager."

Abdu walked back to the table and picked up several of the bamboolike splints. "Let's try a few of these burning under your toenails. Did you ever use these on anybody?"

Carmody swallowed and said, "God forgive me again."

"Yeah? Well, you thought all that was behind you, didn't you? Just goes to show we can't ever get away from our evil deeds; they follow us like a dog scenting an old bone."

Abdu approached from the side, kneeled, and then leaned his weight on Carmody's legs. He pulled one shoe and the sock off. Carmody tried to writhe, but he could not move his legs. He screamed as the splinter was driven up under the nail of his big toe.

132

"Go ahead and yell," Abdu said. "Nobody can hear you through these walls."

He took out a box of Kareenan matches and lit one on the bare stone floor. When he had touched off the splint, he arose.

"That wood's soaked in oil," he said. "It burns like hell, doesn't it?"

The knocker clanged. Abdu whirled and drew his gun from a holster beneath his cloak. The clanging continued for a moment, then stopped. Abdu breathed out a sigh of relief, only to jump when the phone rang.

The priest watched the smoke rise from the slowly creeping fire. Although he had stopped screaming, he felt that he was going to faint. He could not imagine a pain more intense than the one he now felt, but he knew that it would not compare with what he would experience when the fire reached the nerves.

"Stop ringing, damn you!" Abdu said.

"I think they're looking for me," Carmody groaned. "They must have found the officers you knocked out. And they know I haven't left the hotel."

"Well, we'll just let them look. They can't get in here as long as the door's bolted."

Carmody hissed with pain, then said, "And what're you going to do afterward? They'll be waiting for you. Besides, they know this is Mrs. Fratt's room and she's not answering. Also that you are missing from your room. And that you haven't left the hotel. A check is made of everybody entering and leaving, you know."

Abdu frowned and glanced at the phone. He walked to the table and tore off a strip of tape. After securing this over Carmody's mouth, he went to the phone.

Carmody wanted to hear the conversation, but he could not. The fire had begun to feed on the wood under his toe-nail. He could hear nothing but his screams, confined within his mouth by the tape and shrilling higher and higher in his head. The pain had not caused his eyesight to dim, however, and he saw the first thin curl of smoke rise from the steel bolt of the door. Abdu did not see it, for his back was turned, and he was still talking over the phone.

A line appeared on the bolt, spread and flowed. The bolt separated into two pieces. At the same time, Abdu whirled, saw the smoke and the cloven bar, and his lips writhed in what must have been a curse.

The door swung on its pivots; Abdu raised his gun and

fired. A round object flew into the room, bounced toward Abdu, and exploded into a dense cloud of yellow smoke that enveloped him. His body became a silhouette that reached shadow arms upward to clutch at his shadow throat. He fell forward. A second later, Kareenans wearing gas masks entered. One of them hastened to Carmody, and tried to pull the splint out of his toe, only to break off the charred piece. He rose and signaled to another, who produced a hypodermic and jabbed it into Carmody's arm. A few seconds later, blessed oblivion came to him.

He awoke in a strange bed. The pain in his toe and his face was gone. Tand was looking down at him. The relief and the unexpected sight of his friend caused him to burst into tears. Tand was not embarrassed, for Kareenan males wept as easily as terrestrial females. He smiled and patted Carmody's hand.

"You're all right now. You're in my house, safe and sound, for the moment, anyway. We kasered through the door and the bolt just in time. We were lucky. Apparently, Abdu did not discover what we were doing in time to kill you."

"Abdu was just knocked out?"

"Yes, he's alive and being interrogated now."

"He has said anything about any connections with Lieftin and Abog?"

"We used chalarocheil, and he's spilled everything. Abdu made arrangements through Lieftin to have you killed; it was Lieftin's men that tried to murder you outside Mrs. Kri's. However, we're sure that Lieftin not only did this independently of Abog but was careful to conceal his part in the plot against you from Abog. Abog would want to keep you alive, because he and Rilg are depending upon your help in talking Yess out of a universal Night.

"You, my dear friend, were caught in a mesh of cross-webs."

"Is Mrs. Fratt dead?"

"I'm afraid so. Abdu told us how she was killed."

Tand, seeing Carmody flinch, hastened to reassure him. "What else could you do?"

"I know you well enough to know what you're digging for," Carmody said. "You're wondering why I, a man who's passed the Night, would battle so savagely? Why I didn't continue to try to talk Mrs. Fratt out of torturing me when she was so obviously on the point of weakening?"

"That had occurred to me. But I understand why you al-

134

lowed your will to survive to overcome you. A man who's gone through one Night is not 'perfect,' far from it. I've gone through many, and while I'm 'better' each time, I still have a long way to go. Besides, who am I to judge? I might well have done the same thing."

He paused, then said, "But there is one thing I don't understand. You have the power to dissociate your mind from pain. Why didn't you use that power?"

"I tried to," Carmody replied. "And, for the first time, I couldn't."

"Hmmm. I see."

"Something in me cut the wires," the priest said. "It's obvious why. I felt, or the unconscious part of me felt, that I should suffer because of what I'd done to Mrs. Fratt and her son. It wasn't a logical feeling, because my pain wasn't going to alter Mrs. Fratt's situation or feelings or mine, either. But the unconscious has its own logic, as you well know."

He wiggled his big toe. "No pain."

"It'll hurt after the anesthetic wears off. But you should be able to control the pain after that. Unless you are still determined to inflict remorse on yourself."

"I don't think so."

He sat up. He was a little weak and shaky, and, surprisingly, hungry.

"I'd like to eat. What time is it?"

"You're due to see Yess in an hour. Think you can make it?"

"I'll be fine. Now, what are you going to do about Abog and Rilg?"

"That depends on Yess. It's a very complicated situation. It'll take time to figure out what to do and then put a plan into effect. And time is what we lack. By the way, we haven't located Lieftin yet."

Carmody got out of bed. By the time he had eaten, bathed and dressed, he felt his old self again.

Tand was delighted. "I wanted you to look your best when you met your son," he said. "Our son, rather, although I feel that you are actually much more the Father than the rest of us."

"Will the others be there?"

"Not now. Let's go. It'll take longer than usual to get there because of the crowds."

Tand was wrong. Only a few people were on the streets, and these were not as noisy or active as usual.

"I've never seen this before," he said. It must be the worry

135

about Yess' decision. People must be staying home, watching TV in case Yess makes an announcement."

The car drove around to the rear of the enormous temple, a side Carmody had not seen. It lacked the portico with its caryatids and had very few carvings in the niches. Tand parked the car near the entrance and led Carmody to a little door at the southwest corner of the building. A squad of sentinels saluted him, and an officer opened the door for them with a large key that hung on a silver chain from his broad belt.

Beyond the door was a small waiting room with a few tables and chairs and a number of Kareenan and non-Kareenan magazines, books, and record spools. The only other door led to another room which housed the lower end of a narrow staircase of quartz steps and a small graviton cage. This was at the bottom of a shaft carved out of the stone.

Tand and Carmody got into the cage; Tand pressed the start button and the button marked with the ideograph for seven. "I won't go in with you," he said. "Obviously, you won't have to be introduced, even if protocol normally requires it. He's seen your photo. Besides, who else could you be?"

Carmody felt nervous. The cage stopped. Tand swung its gate out, and they stepped into another small anteroom. He fitted a key into the lock of the oval door and turned it. Then he drew a similar key from his beltbag and gave it to Carmody.

"Every Father has one of these."

Carmody hesitated. Tand said, "Go on in. Yess should be in the room beyond the next one. I'll go down below to wait for you."

Carmody nodded and stepped through. He was in a much larger room, lit only by a small lamp. Red drapes covered the wall; a light green carpet, very thick and soft, covered the floor. Although there were no windows, cool air moved past his slightly damp skin. At the opposite wall was another oval door, half-open.

"Come in," said a deep baritone voice in Kareenan.

Carmody entered an even larger room. This had walls covered with light green plaster. Several murals, depicting events from Kareenan mythology, were painted on the walls. The furniture was simple: a table of glossy black wood, several lightly constructed but comfortable-looking chairs, and a bed in a niche. There was also a viewphone, a large TV set, and a tall narrow bookcase at the same glossy wood. The table held recording spools, several books, stationery, and an old-fashioned fountain pen made of polished stone with white and green veins.

Yess was standing by the table. He was a tall man; Carmody's head came no higher than his chest. His superbly muscled body was naked. His black hair looked Terrestrial, but a closer inspection showed a slightly Kareenan featheriness. His face was handsome and also Kareenan, but Carmody felt his throat closing when he saw Mary's features reflected in those of Yess. His ears were like a wolf's; his teeth were a very faint blue. But he had five toes.

A pang welled up in Carmody, drove up through his chest, forced a sob from him, and sprang out as tears. He began weeping violently, and he stumbled to Yess and embraced him. Yess was also weeping.

Yess released himself and sat Carmody down in a chair. He slid open a drawer of the table and took out a handkerchief to wipe his eyes.

"I've looked forward for a long time to this," he said. "Yet I know that it is going to be difficult. We are strangers, and no matter how much we come to know each other, I'm afraid that there will always be a certain barrier between us."

For the first time in his life, Carmody found it difficult to talk. What could he say?

"As you can see, Father," Yess went on, "I am half-Terrestrial, truly your son. And that, by the way, is one of our arguments about the universality of Boontism. Once restricted to this planet, Boontism is destined to spread throughout the universe. Its destiny became manifest the moment I was conceived by an extra-Kareenan mother and Father. Boonta accomplished this for a very specific purpose."

Carmody, feeling better, smiled. "You certainly have one of my characteristics: directness. And I am certain also that you have another: aggressiveness. I can't say I'm altogether happy about the last, though."

Yess smiled, and he sat down in the chair on the other side of the table.

"I'll come to the point then. A question. Why did you, who went through the mystical mating with Boonta, become a convert to another religion? I would have thought that you would be so overwhelmed with a sense of the truth of Boonta and with the experiences of the Night, that you could not have done otherwise than worship Boonta."

"Others, notably my superiors of the Church, have asked me that same question," Carmody replied. "Perhaps, if I'd

137

stayed on Kareen, I might have become a Boontist. But I sincerely believe that a Something—Destiny, Fate, or God— a term I prefer—directed me otherwise. While under observation at Hopkins, I went through an experience, fully as mystical and convincing as anything that happened here. I became convinced, and nothing has happened since then to unconvince me, that the faith I chose was the one for me."

Yess' voice was pleasant, but he was watching Carmody's face very intently.

"You think, then, that Boonta is a false diety?"

"Not at all. Rather, I should say that She is the manifestation the Creator takes on Kareen. She is another aspect. At least, I like to think that. But I really do not know, nor do I think I shall ever be certain. My own Church has made no official declaration, and it may be a long time before it does."

"I am not the least uncertain," Yess said. He reached into the drawer and took out a small bottle and a package.

"The wine is Kareenan; the cigarettes, Terrestrial. I enjoy both. And when I do, I think of my origin. I am no longer Yess, god of Kareen only. I am Yess, the god of all planets."

He spoke matter-of-factly.

"You really believe that?"

"I know."

"Then there's no use arguing," Carmody said. "Not that I intended to do so, anyway. But I'll be frank. I did come here to try to dissuade you from taking a particular step. I—"

"I know why you're here. Your Church has sent you to give me the same arguments that Rilg presented. Rilg, by the way, although he may not know it, is an Algulist. I've been aware of it for a long time, but I've done nothing about it because I never, or rarely, interfere in governmental affairs. Besides, almost all politicians on this planet—and probably on others—are Algulists. Consciously or unconsciously."

"Then you've made up your mind?"

"Last year. I don't intend to make the announcement until the last moment, however. If the people have too much time to think about it, they may revolt.

"Of course, I can't blame them too much. Too many of them know, deep inside them, that they won't make it through the Night. But the time is past for coddling the self-deceivers. If they are truly Algulists behind their façade of Yess worship, they must find out."

"But what about the children?" Carmody said. He knew his face was getting red and that Yess was aware of his anger.

"Life is a spendthrift. Life is a struggle. Some make it;

138

some don't. Boonta gives, but she doesn't take back. She allows things to happen as they happen."

Carmody sat silent overwhelmed with the knowledge that nothing he could say would turn Yess aside.

"After the Night is over and we have reorganized," Yess was saying, "we shall go into an intensive campaign of extra-Kareenan proselytizing. I intend to visit other planets myself."

"Isn't that dangerous?" Carmody said. "If you're assassinated by some religious fanatic on another planet, you'll be discredited."

"Not so. Another Yess will appear. That a Yess can be killed will no more invalidate his divinity than the killing of Christ did His."

"Next you'll be telling me that planets do have their own local saviors, good enough in their own way but only temporary substitutes until the oversavior comes along—you."

"Exactly," Yess replied. "It's the evolution of the divine. Just as the New Testament was added to the Old Testament to make a new book, and as the Book of Mormon and the Koran and the Keys to Science and Health were sequels to the Bible, so another Book will come into being and supersede all of them.

"I am dictating the Book of Light. It will be finished presently. In it is a compressed history of Boonta and her peoples. It also presents in organized and authentic form the tenets of our religion. And it does what no other scriptures have ever dared. It makes a detailed prophecy of things to come. This is not given in vague symbolic form, so that a thousand different interpretations are possible. It is clean and specific.

"When this Book is translated into the many tongues of the galaxies and made available everywhere, it will be our greatest missionary."

Yess looked across the table into Carmody's eyes, and Carmody felt the hairs on the back of his neck rise. It was the aura, though much attenuated, that he had felt when he went into the Temple with the other Fathers for the birth of Yess—when Boonta had made Her presence known.

Abruptly, the feeling stopped. Yess rose and said, "I will see you, Father."

Carmody stood up also. "Am I free to make your decision known?"

"No. You will say nothing of it."

Yess strode around the table, embraced Carmody and kissed him. "Do not grieve, Father. There are things beyond

139

your understanding. You must accept them, just as you accepted the things of the Night and my conception by a creature of your mind."

"I would like to do so," Carmody replied. "But I cannot accept needless suffering and death."

"They are not needless. Boonta be with you."

"And God with you—son."

Tand greeted the priest as he entered the waiting room on the ground floor. "How did it go, John? How do you feel?"

"Downcast. And troubled. I feel somewhat like an actor who has walked onto the stage only to find himself in the wrong theater and the wrong play."

"You've completed your mission. Why don't you go home?"

"I don't know why, but I can't. Something tells me I have unfinished business here. Perhaps it's to find out the truth, if that's possible. I'll tell you one thing. Yess' theory of one universal savior disturbs me very much. Are divine truths revealed little by little as sentients become ready for them? And is Yess about to reveal one, a valid one?"

Carmody went home and to bed. He slept until late in the morning, an event rare for him. When he went down to the hotel dining room for breakfast, he found it empty of all non-Kareenans except for a number of Terrestrial converts to Boontism. He ate a sad breakfast alone. Just before he finished, he was interrupted by a priest of Boonta.

Carmody looked up at the green robes and peacocktail-like headdress, and it was a few seconds before he recognized Skelder.

Carmody stood up and joyfully threw his arms around him. It was an indication of the change in the once dour and withdrawn priest that he responded as eagerly.

"I wanted to see you before the Night started," Skelder said. "After that, who knows?"

"There's no need for me to ask if you still think you made the right choice?" Carmody said.

"No. I'm perfectly happy about my decision. Never regretted it. And you?"

"Same here. Well, shall we sit down and talk?"

"I'd like to," Skelder said, "but I must be at the Temple. Yess is going to make the announcement at noon, you know."

"No, I didn't. What then?"

"What happens is in the hands of Boonta. Tand told me that you know much about events behind the scenes. So, you must know that we wouldn't be surprised if Rilg tried to keep

Yess from making the public announcement. Not that he'd dare lay hands on Yess—officially, anyway. But he could try to cut off the electrical power or jam the broadcast."

"He must be desperate."

"He is. Well, I must be off. Oh, yes, Tand said that Lieftin is still at large. And he must be desperate, too. The last ship has left, he can't get off. However, he may expect to be put to Sleep during the Night and so escape its effects. We think he'll try whatever he has planned before the broadcast. Maybe that is what Rilg is hoping for."

Skelder said goodby and left in a swirl of long green robes. Carmody signed the government credit slip for his breakfast and went out into the street. He was unaccompanied, since there no longer seemed any reason to guard him. Many people were in the streets. They stood silently on the corners by the large public TV screens, evidently awaiting Yess. Many had removed their masks.

Carmody tried to talk to some of those standing on the sidewalk in front of the hotel. After several attempts, he gave up. They not only did not want to talk to him, they scowled and turned away or muttered under their breaths.

After standing around the lobby for a while, he went back to his room. He tried without success to get interested in a book on Kareenan history. Noon came, and with a sense of relief he turned on the TV. The announcer made a short and familiar speech. Apparently, despite the advances of science on both Earth and Kareen, technical difficulties could still be encountered. If the viewer would be patient, these would be remedied within a very short time. Meanwhile, here was an important . . .

A half-hour passed with several more assurances and a brief documentary about the landing of the first Earthman on Kareen. By then, Carmody knew that something must be wrong. He tried to call Tand, but got a busy signal. Another half-hour went by with more assurances and documentaries that had nothing to do with the appearance of Yess. He called Tand three more times, only to get more busy signals. By then, he assumed, the phone system was jammed with calls from people wanting to know what was wrong.

Suddenly, the announcer said, "People of Kareen, your god!"

Yess came into view, visible from the waist up. He smiled and said, "My beloved ones, I . . ."

The screen went blank. Carmody swore. He shot the bolt to the door, ran down the hall, and down the fourteen flights of stairs to the lobby. This was jammed with people talking loudly. Carmody grabbed a bellhop and said, "The station? The TV station? Is it near?"

"Three blocks, Father. East," the bellhop replied. He seemed dazed.

Carmody pushed through the mob and ran out the door. There were many in the street now, all with shocked expressions. A large number were speaking incoherently. They also knew that something had happened to their god. And, if they had been resenting or fearing what he was going to say, they had lost that feeling. They were panicky or awestruck, numb or outraged. They did not oppose the passage of the little Earthman who flew by them, but they stared after him.

Before he was within a block of the TV building, Carmody saw the clouds of smoke boiling out of the windows on the first two floors. A milling crowd impeded the efforts of policemen and ambulance men to enter. Carmody shoved against the backs of those in his way, but he could not move them.

A hand tapped Carmody's shoulder. He whirled and saw Tand.

"What happened?" he demanded.

"Lieftin must have planted explosives so cleverly that the police couldn't find them," Tand said. "Or else they did not want to find them. The broadcast was held up for an hour while a search was made through the station for bombs. Then Yess came on, and . . . You saw the screen go blank. I would have been with him if my car had not collided with another. I wasn't hurt, but my chauffeur was."

He looked at the building. "Do you suppose he could be dead?"

"I don't know," Carmody said. "What's that?"

A cry had arisen. Suddenly, as if an invisible engine had moved through them, the crowd parted. Yess, blackened with smoke and bleeding in several places but otherwise unharmed, walked through.

He signaled to Tand, who came running with Carmody after him.

"Get a car and get me to Station Fuurdal," Yess said.

Tand said, "I have a car near here. It's not mine; mine was wrecked. Come."

He led them down the street while the people stepped back. All were weeping with joy at seeing their god alive; some ran up, fell on their knees, and tried to kiss Yess' hand. He waved them away, smiling, and strode on. Within a minute, the three, Tand driving, were on their way to the TV

142

station.

"I do not understand how Lieftin, or whoever did this, managed to conceal explosives," Yess said. "The police and the priests went through every piece of equipment, anything that could hide a bomb. Strangely enough, it was Abog who insisted that the broadcast be held up until the building could be examined."

"He may have wanted to supply the government with an alibi," Carmody said.

"Probably. He was not in the building when the bomb went off. Everybody around me was killed or badly hurt. The Fathers died. You and Carmody are the only ones alive now."

Yess wept. Then, without a trace of the emotion he must still be feeling, he said, "Call your best men, Tand. We may need a bodyguard to get back to the Temple."

Tand picked up the carphone and began to make calls. By the time they stopped in front of their destination, he had made sure that fifty armed men would shortly be available. Moreover, a number of armed priests would follow them.

Carmody followed the two into the building, but he did not go into the room from which Yess would make his announcement. He felt that Yess was not safe from further attempts. If anybody came through this room to harm Yess, he would have to deal with Carmody.

Only seconds after Yess had gone into the caster, gunshots sounded in the hall. A Kareenan burst into the room, a pistol in his hand. Carmody, standing to one side, hit him over the head with a bronze statuette.

After picking up the weapon dropped by the unconscious man and shoving it in his belt, he went out into the hall. Three dead would-be assassins and two dead and two wounded policemen sprawled on the floor. A station employee was cowering behind a chair. Carmody pulled him out and sent him to call the ambulance. Then he returned to the room to ready himself again.

Ten minutes later Yess and Tand came out of the caster, both looking grave.

"It is done," Yess said. "Now, what Boonta lets fall must fall."

On the way back to the Temple, the people in the street stepped back for the armed escort of Yess. Carmody, gazing out at the faces and masks, suddenly cried out, "Stop the car!"

Yess ordered the chauffeur to stop and turned to ask Carmody what the matter was, but the little Earthman was al-

143

ready off.

Carmody had seen a masked man whose walk made him sure it was Lieftin. Afraid that Lieftin might get away, he dashed off without telling anybody what he was after. He shouted, "Lieftin! You're under arrest!" not realizing in his excitement that the others had not followed him.

The man turned and ran. For a second Carmody lost sight of him in the crowd; then he saw him plunge into the entrance of a clothing shop. He followed. It was a large place, one that catered to a wealthy clientele. A single saleswoman was standing with her face pressed against the window, presumably to watch Yess when he came by. Carmody shouted at her, and she jumped. He could see by her startled expression that she had not seen Lieftin enter the shop. Ignoring her questions, he went to the back of the room. There were three doors. He took the first one on the left, went through several rooms and came out in the alley. There was no one there. As he turned to reenter the shop, there was a footstep behind him and pain exploded in his head.

When he came to, he found himself sprawled on the rough cobblestones of the alley. There was a tender lump over his ear. The streets around him were quiet; the Night had begun.

He was appalled at what he saw on the streets. Corpses lay in all directions as far as he could see. There were men, women, and children among them, torn by bullets and knives, some cut in half by kaser beams. A truck lay on its side with its kaser tube blown apart by a bomb, probably dropped from a window above. The soldiers who had manned the kaser were dead.

Blood ran in a shallow stream down the gutters.

Carmody picked up a gun, checked its clip, and hurriedly set off down the street. Before he had gone far, he grew dizzy and hot; his sight blurred. Then the flicker of the sun, effective even around the curve of the planet, had passed.

Several blocks down the street, he found the Kareenan drive-stick equivalent of a motorcycle on its side. It was still operable, even though part of the seat had been blown off, along with its rider. It was a twisting, weaving course he had to take to avoid running over the many corpses, but he managed it. Then, going around a corner, the motorcycle skidded on something slippery, hit the curb, and threw him across the sidewalk. He struck the side of the building hard, but he was not hurt so badly that he could not get up. The cycle's front wheel was too bent for him to continue on it, so he limped away.

As he neared the Temple of Boonta, he heard the sound of firing and saw men running. He ducked into an office, crouched down behind the broken window and watched. Ahead of the mob came one man, a thin fellow in the rags of a robe. He was running as fast as his long legs could pump, but he was winded and sobbing for breath.

Carmody stood up and called to the man. Gunshots drowned out his voice. Lifted and hurled forward by the bullets, the man fell on his face.

By the still-operating streetlights, Carmody saw that the man was Skelder.

So, this was for Skelder the end of the Night that had begun so many years ago.

A bullet crashed through the broken window. Carmody turned and ran through the shadowy interior into the alley.

Footsteps pounded close behind him. Carmody dropped on all fours. The pursuer fell over him, and Carmody raised his gun to fire.

"Don't shoot! It's me, Tand!"

Carmody lowered the gun again, shaking with relief. Tand arose, lobbed something over Carmody toward the rear exit of the office. He pushed Carmody down, and both cowered flat on the pavement of the alley. There was a deafening roar and a blast of air that tore at their clothes.

Both jumped up and ran on down the alley to the next open door. There, between gasps for breath, they talked.

"I was hiding in the office when you entered," Tand said. "I didn't know who you were, you were just a silhouette. But when you turned, I saw enough of your profile to recognize you. I ran after you . . ."

"Strange that the three of us should converge at the same spot," Carmody said. "That was Skelder who died outside the shop."

Tand made the circular sign. "Well, his last years were happy ones. I was looking for you when the riots broke out, and I had to take refuge. The Temple is surrounded by Algulists, but they're a somewhat disorganized bunch. Every time there's a flicker, fighting breaks out among them."

"How can we get in?" Carmody said.

"I know a way. But we have to be very careful not to reveal it. If the Enemy also found it, they could surprise those within the Temple."

They left the shop, and, hugging the wall, walked only another block. Tand led the priest into a market that had been looted. There were four dead in the aisles or behind counters, one of them a child. Tand grimaced and went into the back offices, where a headless corpse sprawled across a desk. He went through a doorway behind the desk into a large closet. This had been a stockroom, but the papers and pens had been strewn about, typewriters and office equipment smashed.

Carmody followed the Kareenan behind a pile of large wooden boxes, some of which had been ripped open. Tand stopped, felt over the naked stone blocks of the wall, and pressed. A large block at the bottom of the wall slid inward. He got down on his hands and knees and crawled through the opening with the Earthman behind him. The interior was dark except for the light coming in through the opening. Tand stood up and did something; the block moved back to its former position.

Light flooded the place. Tand removed his hand from a plate set in the wall. They were in a small room at the end of which was a narrow archway.

"The tunnel is narrow and low," Tand said, "and it dips sharply downward. There are enough eternalights for us to see our way. Follow me, but not too closely. I may stop suddenly, and I don't want you bumping into me and knocking me forward. It could be fatal for both of us."

As Carmody followed Tand, he looked beyond and ahead of him and saw that there were only very dim footprints in the thick dust. He asked Tand about it.

"I've never been here myself, but I've studied maps of this tunnel and of others. Only Yess, the Fathers, and the highest priests and priestesses know of it, only those who've passed the Night. Even so . . ."

Tand stopped and held up his hand. Carmody examined the wall and floor ahead of them but could see nothing unusual.

"What is it?"

Tand indicated one of the bulbs on the ceiling. "See that? It has a small black spot on it that looks like dirt. It's a sign. Now, watch me, then do as I do."

Tand drew a line in the dust before him, then backed up ten steps, crouched and began to run. Just before he came to the line in the dust, he veered and ran on the curving side of the tunnel, his momentum allowing him to do so for several meters. When he had come down off the wall and back onto the floor, he slowed and stopped.

He turned to Carmody. "All right, come on. Don't slip."

Carmody sprinted after him. After joining Tand, he said,

"What would have happened if we had just walked across the floor at that spot?"

"Nothing necessarily fatal," Tand replied. "The ceiling above that point, which looks like solid stone, is a trap door. It would open, and a great quantity of sticky jelly would drop and imprison you. At the same time, an alarm would go off in the Temple and a light on a control board, indicating the alarm location, would be illuminated. You'd be held fast until the Temple guards came to dissolve the jelly. You might not be alive; it would depend on whether the jelly happened to cover your nostrils and mouth."

They continued for fifty meters. After that the tunnel began to slant sharply upward. At its top, they came to an iron door. Tand pulled a key from his beltbag and inserted it, not in the keyhole in the door but in a hole to one side in the wall. The door swung open.

They stepped into a small room, bare of furniture and with thick dust on the floor. Another door, opened with the same wall key, permitted access to yet another small room. A third door, swinging on pivots as the hotel doors did, gave them entrance to a hall the floor of which was dusty. Again, the key unlocked another door, and they were in the anteroom in which Carmody had been before. It was the one with the elevator cage that had taken him up to meet Yess.

The door swung shut behind them and seemed to be one piece with the wall.

"Get in," Tand said. The cage rose. At the top of the shaft, they left the cage and walked down a broad corridor for at least half a kilometer. There were many doors on both sides, all shut. At the end of the passageway, they came to another elevator. It took them back down to the ground floor. Two more rooms had to be crossed, and then they were in the great room where, so many years ago, Carmody had murdered the old Yess.

The new Yess was there. He stopped talking to the Fathers and priests and priestesses gathered around him to greet the two newcomers. "I had not yet given up hope that you were alive and could get here. But I was beginning to have doubts."

"What's the situation?" Tand said.

"Rilg and his Algulists are besieging us. They have some heavy artillery and kasers, but they haven't used them against the Temple, and I doubt that they will. Their war is with me; they would not dare to do too much damage to the house of the Great Mother Herself. But they are preventing anybody from entering or leaving. I think they plan to attack later in the Night."

Yess placed his hand on the priest's shoulder and said, "Come to my rooms, Father. I have something I want to show you."

Tand shouted, "Look out!" He was pointing upward.

Lieftin was standing in the gallery above. He was against the railing and had a bazooka on his shoulder aimed at Yess.

Carmody drew his gun and fired.

Only later was he able to reconstruct what had happened. A blast of fire and smoke covered Lieftin. The roaring air knocked Carmody and all those around him, except Yess, off their feet. Carmody arose, stunned, still unable to perceive that Lieftin was somehow gone. But his senses cleared, and he could see that the gallery was essentially the same as before Lieftin had appeared, except for a big red spot, like the shadow of a ragged octopus, covering some carved stone benches.

He walked up the flight of steps that led to the gallery and examined the benches. The twisted bazooka, one end ripped off, lay under a bench. A few scraps of skin, blood, and smashed bones were all that remained of Lieftin.

Tand, who had followed him, said, "I think your bullet struck the missile just as it came out of the tube. It exploded, and—well, you see the result."

"I was aiming at him, not the tube," Carmody said. "It was a lucky shot, just plain dumb luck."

"Are you sure?" Tand said. "I'm not."

"You mean that someone—Yess or Boonta?—guided my aim?"

Tand shrugged and said, "Not the Mother." He made the circular sign. "She would not take sides. But Yess . . . who knows? He will not say."

"It was chance."

"As you will. There's no way of proving or disproving it."

Tand went up to the top row of benches and out through an archway. Carmody, going after him, found him looking into a doorway cut in the stone of the wall.

"Lieftin, or, those who hired him, found another one of our secret entrances," Tand said. "It was to be expected. I wonder how long they've known about it?"

"Won't they be using it again when they find Lieftin has failed?"

"I doubt they'll try it. They banked on one man getting through, which was wise of them, for a number might have tripped off the alarms. And they know we'll not allow them to use the same tunnels again. I'm going now to make sure they're all closed."

Tand strode off. Carmody returned to Yess, who repeated his invitation to go to his rooms. When they arrived, Yess pulled a dicspool from a drawer of his desk.

"I dictated this an hour ago. It's the last chapter of the Book of Light. I do not know myself what it says, for I was in the presence of the Mother. She talked, and I was Her voice."

He handed the spool to Carmody. "Take it with you; run it off. When the Night is ended, see if what I have said has not come true."

"You predicted the course of events to come?"

"In full detail."

"How do you know this if you can't remember what you said?"

Yess smiled. "I *know*."

Carmody put the spool in the beltbag. "Why do you give it to me? Do you expect something to happen to you?"

"I don't know anything except that you were to get the last chapter. Will you promise that you'll have it published?"

"Do you realize what you're asking? I'm a priest of a Church that is threatened by your religion. Why should I have it published?"

"Because you are the one who is entrusted with it. That's all I am able to tell you."

Carmody said, "I can't promise anything. I'd have to consult with my superiors first. They will undoubtedly want to hear it themselves, and what they will do with it after that I can't say."

"Very well. But at least promise me that you'll listen to it before anyone does. Then you may act as you see fit."

"Very well. Now I'd like to be alone for a while. The only place is the roof top. How can I get to there?"

Yess gave him directions. As Carmody started to leave, Yess embraced and kissed him. "You are my Father," Yess whispered.

"In one way I am," Carmody said. "But I wonder what a scientific comparison of blood and cell types would show? Tell me, do you feel lonely? Do you think you might have made a terrible mistake by commanding all to go through the Night?"

"I am alone but not lonely. Don't mistake my expression of love for you as a weakness or cry for help. I am Yess, a being you cannot understand, one that only another Yess could understand. Or, which may seem strange to you, an Algul."

149

Yess walked away. Carmody watched him and thought of what a splendid being, physically, the naked god was. And he thought of the impossibility of Yess' existence. Only a miracle, or some form of supernatural power, could have created him.

This was the overpowering factor in the spread of Boontism; this was what made it so dangerous to all other religions, not just those of Earth alone.

When he stepped out of the gravcage onto the rooftop, Carmody was startled. Subconsciously, he must have expected an unrelieved flatness. Most large buildings of the Federation had level and unobstructed roofs to receive aircraft. But he had forgotten that he was not only on the planet of Dante's Joy but on the high place of the Temple of Boonta Herself. And before, behind, below and above was a maelstrom of stone shapes, a mimetomantic nightmare.

Originally, the rooftop must have been meters-thick, a solid slab of marble webbed with many colors. From it some mad Titan had chiseled an inferno of writhing figures. And he must have started from the very spot on which Carmody stood, since the flow and rush and swirl of rock was outward in every direction from this center, as if the figures were waves twisted by the force of a whirlpool and he was at the bottom of a hole created by the vortex in the marble sea.

Nevertheless, despite the first impression of an impenetrable host, there were avenues, and through one of these Carmody made a slow and cautious progress toward the edge of the rooftop.

Savage and long-necked and crawling things, flat-tailed, tentacled, and flippered, jostled each other and turned to bite at one another or even at themselves. Many were coiled in furious combat or even more furious copulation, in disregard of difference of kind.

Carmody had to duck under a huge head barring his path. The long teeth projecting downward tugged against the back of his cloak. Abruptly, he was in a gigantomachy of land monsters. These, like the thalassic things behind him, were eating or chasing each other or mating with a frenzy that only a master could have evoked from the inanimate marble. Yet, the faces of the creatures, no matter how savage, contained more intelligence and, somehow, more a sense of striving forward than those of the beasts Carmody had first encountered.

When these ceased, there was a group of lonely statues, of past Yesses and Alguls. These also had jewels for eyes, set in such a fashion that they seemed to follow Carmody as he passed their owners. One of the Alguls sent a chill through Carmody, so evil was his stare.

He hurried past the Algul to the rampart at the edge of the roof, near the statue of a Yess. This, too, gave him a start and a chill, since he recognized the features of the god he had murdered so many years ago. Only now, it did not seem so long ago. It was as if he had just left him, because Yess held a half-eaten candle in his hand and there was a red wound upon his forehead and one ear was half shot off. Carmody tried to ignore the reminder of the man he had once been.

He looked out over the ramparts at the city of Rak. Around the horizon, distant and huge fires burned. The haze above the flames was a light purple, and it seemed to coil and writhe. Snakes, octopuses, rags of faces appeared, dissolved, and re-formed into new images. The fires, he knew, were coming from the recently built suburbs surrounding the massive stone heart of the old city. The wooden houses were burning to the ground, and the firemen were dead, fighting for their lives and souls, or else had helped touch off the flames themselves.

From far below, cries rose. There were screams, shouts, bellows, and, now and then, the punctuation marks of small-arms. The firing from the besieging Algulists immediately below had ceased. Perhaps they had turned on each other and were fighting with the weapons they had been born with—or those they had developed in the metamorphoses the Night sometimes brought.

The flicker of the sun around the curve of the planet gripped him then, as if the star's great hands had twisted a cord around him and pulled both ends. He felt squeezed, and he thought he would burst.

"John Carmody!" wailed a voice, far off and plaintive. "Evil John Carmody!"

It was the voice of Mrs. Fratt.

He looked to his right, for it sounded as if she stood somewhere at the distant end of the rooftop. But there was no one there.

"Carmody! I want my son back! My eyes!"

He began shaking, for he fully expected her to materialize out of the air as Mary had done. But there was no hardening of the atmosphere, only the mauve flickerings.

Again the voice keened. "You are a killer, John Carmody! You began as one and you end as one!"

"Mrs. Fratt," he said aloud, then he stopped. He left the roof and went down in the gravcage to the room in which

151

Lieftin had died.

The others were sitting on chairs around a great round table that had not been there before.

Carmody asked Yess for permission to speak and told them of the voice.

"You feel guilty because of Mrs. Fratt," Yess said. "You know that at the time you should have continued to try to talk her out of her vengeance. But you panicked and allowed your old reflexes to take over."

"I couldn't go on any longer with persuasion," the priest said heatedly. "She was not alone. Abdu would have insisted she carry through or, if she had refused, he would have carried it through himself."

"If you believed that in your innermost self, you would not now be hearing Mrs. Fratt," Yess replied.

"I am not a saint!" Carmody said loudly.

Yess did not reply. There was silence for a minute.

The men and women at the table brooded with their eyes fixed on their wine cups and the half-eaten cakes made in the image of the Seven Fathers. The priests and priestesses sitting on one side of the table or scattered throughout the huge chamber were mute or else conversed in whispers.

Finally, Tand raised his head and spoke.

"Don't despair, John. All of us who have gone through more than one Night have experienced these things. We call them 'residues.' You may go through seven Nights and still not be cleansed of them.

"In fact, and I do not say this to frighten you but to acquaint you with reality, which is in essence a variety of potentialities . . ."

He stopped, cleared his throat, and smiled. "I'll try not to be too long-winded. There have been cases, exceedingly rare, of what we call retroconversion. The most famous, infamous rather, is that of Ruugro. He was one of the Fathers of the previous Yess. During the seventh Night after the previous Yess was conceived, Ruugro switched over. No one knows why or how, but he became an Algulist. And he almost effected the birth of a new Algul before he was killed."

"Then we're never safe?" Carmody said.

"Every breath of life draws in good and evil," Yess said. "Strife accompanies a man with each step. There is no letup."

"Has a Yess ever become an Algul?" the bishop said.

"Never," Yess replied. "But then the sons of Boonta, though they may die, are not mortal."

As the long Night wore on, Carmody tried to sort out his

thoughts about Yess, and found that he could not. How could the god of "good," if he were what he claimed to be, cause this devastation? He was roused from his thoughts by a priest who spoke to Yess. "Son of Boonta, the Algulists are massing before the Temple. They may be getting ready to attack."

Yess nodded and went to the table on which stood the golden candlestick holder in the form of a coiling serpent. The candle that should have been there was missing. That long time ago, Carmody had so thoroughly destroyed the body of the murdered Yess with his panpyric, only a few ashes had been left. These had been mixed with the wax of the trogur bird, but the present Yess ha deaten all of the tiny candle several Nights before.

Seeing the empty holder, Carmody felt guilty for a moment. He was aware that the Kareenans thought the new Yess imbibed divinity and spiritual power from eating the ashes of the old Yess and that Carmody's act had robbed them of this sacrament. Yet, though he knew that the Kareenans were conscious of what he had done and must resent the act, he had not heard a word of reproach.

Yess, standing by the table, touched the candleholder with his hand as if he thought he would, at least, derive some strength from its former associations. He raised his head, shut his eyes, and began to chant. He prayed thus in the ancient language permitted to the gods alone.

Tand held one of Carmody's hands and a priestess held the other. All except Yess were linked thus. They stood side by side, the entire line forming a crescent whose center was behind Yess and whose horns curved outward past him and then a little inward. From the beginning of the chanting, Carmody had felt a thrill run through his hands, up his arms and across his body, like a weak electrical current. As Yess continued, his voice louder and louder and the phrases seeming to become longer and longer, the cold prickling built up in Carmody. The torches on the walls flickered more and more, or seemed to do so. However, when he concentrated on a single torch, it burned steadily. The air in the upper reaches of the chamber became several shades darker, the light-purple hue intensifying unevenly until bars and coils formed. These shifted a little, writhed slowly, bent downward, twisted upward. The room became colder so suddenly that it seemed as if the heat were being driven out by something threatening.

Sweat trickled down Carmody's armpits and over his ribs. The iciness and the static charge—the aura of panic—grew stronger. His heart thudded, and his legs quivered. He felt that the walls were about to peel away in a flood of utterly cold light—light that would not only blind his eyes, but would fill the deepest and darkest recesses of his body and that entity he called his soul so full of icy luminescence that reason and the senses could not tolerate it.

"Steady!" Tand murmured. "I, too, feel it, but you must stand! If you don't, you are lost! And so are we! Boonta does not condone weakness!"

The door swung open, and a mob of Kareenans rushed in. Most of them were in their original humanoid form, but a few had metamorphosed. Their leader, a man Carmody did not recognize, had two tigerlike canines projecting over his lower lip, and a long nose hardened into a leathery sharp-tipped beak. He held a huge sword that dripped with blood. He raised it above his head and opened his mouth to shout. Then he, and all those with him froze. His arms stayed up, the sword fell from his hands and clattered on the floor.

Yess went on chanting. Those in the crescent let go each other's hands, went to the immobilized men and women, took their weapons and dispassionately slew them. Only when the last one lay dead did they cease. Carmody alone took no part in the slaughter, though he had felt the desire to kill.

Yess stopped chanting. Slowly, too slowly for Carmody, the Presence withdrew.

The god examined the bodies. He shook his head.

"Rilg and Abog are not here. They must still be outside, waiting until the Seven Fathers of Algul have gathered. They sent these to test the temper of the Mother. She favors us at this moment. Next time, they will hope the Mother will allow them to kill me. Then, and only then, can Algul be conceived and born."

Carmody left the room to go back up to the rooftop again. There he prayed, but he felt that the strange stars seen so dimly through the coiling haze were not those his God had made. He could not shake the feeling of desolation that came over him. Was it possible that there could be more than one God, a multitude of Creators?

Perhaps Yess was right. There were local saviors, and there was also an oversavior. Once the oversavior appeared, the locals must go. This would not mean that Carmody's own religion was false; it was true as far as it had gone. Now another aspect was revealed, and one more bit of truth was added to the jigsaw puzzle of the universe.

"Help me in my doubt!" he cried out.

A star fell through the purple. Far below, something huge

laughed and laughed.

He paid no attention to either. He had seen many meteors in the Kareenan sky before, and he knew that it was only a coincidence that the monster was laughing. Besides, if he were superstitious enough to grasp at anything for a sign or an omen, one had canceled out the other.

No, it was an inward sign he wanted. But there was no answer, within or without.

Suddenly, shouts rose from below. Guns fired. Carmody whirled and ran to the gravcage. He started downward, but as he did so, bullets exploded against the bottom of the cage. Carmody threw himself over the waist-high fence and onto the floor that the cage was passing. There were more shouts from below, then screams. The gunfire ceased and was followed by a crashing sound.

He looked down the shaft and saw the cage wrecked on the bottom floor. Several bodies were smashed between it and the wall; legs and arms protruded from beneath the shattered metal.

Firing broke out somewhere else. Yess and his disciples were not all dead. Perhaps the invaders could be driven out again. He ran toward the firing, lost it because of the thick stone walls, and decided to move more cautiously. After a moment, he heard the battle again. At the end of a corridor, he found Tand and some priests exchanging shots with the Algulists along a winding staircase. The Enemy were poking gun barrels around the corners and firing blindly up the stairs.

Joining Tand, Carmody said, "Do you think they have kasers?"

"If they had them, they'd be using them."

"Where's Yess?"

"In his apartment." Tand looked at his wristwatch. "The Night will soon be ended."

He hesitated. "I don't understand it."

"Understand what?"

"How they can be so strong and in the House of Boonta. Well, let them profane it. When the Night is over, Boonta will catch them like rats in a trap."

There was an explosion halfway up the staircase. The defenders reeled back before the ear-stunning blast of air and smoke that followed. Shouts came through the smoke, and the Algulists stumbled upon them through the clouds. The fighting was swift and savage, but the Algulists were killed.

Tand, Carmody, and three priests were left standing. They

ran up the staircase to the next floor and took positions. Two self-propelled grenades landed near and began spitting greenish smoke.

Tand threw a grenade toward those on the stairs, and the explosion hurled the gas-expellers back down. Immediately after, Tand ordered Carmody and the priests to retreat to the next floor.

There Yess appeared with twenty-eight priests and priestesses.

"There are too many," he said. "They'll be coming in from all sides. We must make a stand on the rooftop."

"What about fliers?" Carmody said. "Won't we be vulnerable there?"

Tand said, "I imagine that fliers, like kasers, have all been wrecked."

Yess led the way slowly and with dignity. Carmody, sweating and expecting at any time to be attacked from the rear, wished that they would hurry.

When they reached the roof, he helped the others set up some furniture they had brought as barricades on the seven stairs that gave access to the roof. Yess strode back and forth, between the savage stone figures, while the others worked. Now and then, he looked up at the strands of haze floating above. They were beginning to pale, and the sun could be seen as a great milky globe.

"Boonta will be making Her appearance soon," Tand said to Carmody. "Then we will go down and see what we must do to rebuild our world."

Yess had stopped. His eyes were turned upward, but his head was cocked as if he were listening.

"Mother is here."

His features twisted with anguish. He cried out, "I have not called Her yet! But She comes!"

The rest were silent. One of the priests, white-faced, crooked a finger at them. Carmody stood behind the man who had summoned them and listened. Far off, faintly up the stairwell, the sound of singing arose. The words were not intelligible, but the tone was triumphant.

"They are hailing the birth of Algul!" Tand said.

He looked at Yess. "But that is impossible! You are still living!"

Yess replied, "Be quiet. Listen."

The singing had stopped. There were no more sounds from below, and none came from the city outside the Temple. Tand opened his mouth, closed it when Yess motioned for silence. Several minutes passed while Carmody wondered what Yess was listening for.

A moment later, his question was answered. Weakly at first, then stronger, a baby wailed.

Yess exhaled slowly and deeply. "Aah!"

A male Kareenan voice came up to them. "Listen, fallen god, and you who serve him. Listen. The newly born son of Boonta, Algul, cries your doom! Listen!"

Yess shouted, "Stand where we may see you. Let me see my brother!"

There was a laugh. The Algulist shouted back, "Do you think I am a fool? You would kill me and, far worse, the infant Algul!"

"That's Abog's voice," Tand said. He shouted, "Abog! You spirit of evil! Where is your leader, Rilg?"

"I killed him during the second attack! The fool is dead now, and I am the chief of the Fathers who have survived!"

"Much good may it do you!" Tand shouted. "Go, and take your abominations with you! You will not live long to enjoy them!"

There was another laugh. The wailing of the baby receded and was gone.

Those on the rooftop turned to look at Yess. His face was pale as the rising sun. He said, "This is the first time since the beginning, the first time that Algul and I have lived at the same time."

He spoke to Carmody. "It was a fateful day that you came to our world, Father. You were the first Earthman ever to pass through the entire Night. You were also the first Earthman to become a Father. Since then, things have not been the same on Kareen. Now Night is ended, and the struggle should be over. The course of the next seven years should be plain. But he, my evil brother, is born! And I live!"

"Son of Boonta," Tand said, "what shall we do now?"

Yess turned and walked away. Carmody followed him and said, "Son, what can we do? What can I do?"

Yess stopped and faced him. "Perhaps you and your Church have won this battle, just as Algul has won it. We are outnumbered, and we cannot continue to occupy this roof."

"How do you know they outnumber us?" Carmody asked.

"Look down there," Yess directed.

Carmody leaned over the rampart to examine the street. He gasped, for he saw thousands of men and women, and even a few children. As he watched, he heard them break into song.

"Where are my worshipers?" Yess said.

"Don't give up hope," Carmody replied. He took a small metal case from his beltbag, pushed a button and began to speak. There was no response. At first; then a voice came from the transceiver. Carmody looked up. The sun was shining on a huge metal hemisphere slowly descending toward the spaceport some twenty kilometers away.

"The *Argus*," he said, "a Federation astrophysical research ship. It's been in orbit while the crew and its scientists Slept. Now, they've come back to investigate the aftermath of the Night. They'll answer our call for help, I'm sure. We'll have a way of escape from this roof."

The vessel hovered, then moved toward the Temple. A minute later, its immense flat belly was half a kilometer above the rooftop. A port opened, and a gravsled came through. Within minutes, Yess, Carmody, Tand, and the priests and priestesses were aboard the *Argus*.

An hour later, the ship landed near the beach on the western shore of the continent.

John Carmody said goodby to Yess just before he and his disciples left the ship.

"I will take up the struggle here," Yess said. "This place is far enough from Algul to give me time to organize before he finds out where I am and sends his killers."

"I'd stay with you," the priest replied. "But I must report to my superiors in Rome, and then I must go where they send me."

Yess smiled. "Ah, and what will your report say?"

"Only the truth. Rather, what I heard and saw, which is only a small facet of the truth. But I must tell you this. I am going to give my honest opinion, which is that Boontism is not all it claims to be. It is not the super religion which will displace all others. It will not displace my Church or any firm Christian faith. It may lure many converts, but Boontism is not the true, the universal, faith."

"Why do you say that?" Yess asked, still smiling.

"Would a true god be defeated by the forces of evil? Or, would a 'good' god commit what is, to me at least, such an evil act as your commandment that all go through the Night?"

"I am the Son of the Creatrix," Yess replied, "as Christ was the Son of the Creator. Yet, I am no more omnipotent or omniscient than Christ was in His fleshly incarnation. Nor am I perfect or absolutely 'good.' Remember that it was your own Christ who reproached a man for calling Him good. He said that He was not good; only God was good.

"I am not the Mother Boonta. But I am Her right-hand son, and the right hand is the favored hand. I believe that

I am destined to win—for a long while anyway. I will win, not only here but on all other worlds. Mother has permitted this seeming victory by Algul for reasons of Her own. I will find out in due time.

"Of course, She may be truly indifferent to the outcome, in which case it is entirely up to me. If so, I am confident. Do not think that, because Kareenan civilization has been wrecked and evil has gained the field, that Boontism will be out of the galactic picture for a long time to come. Surprising things may come of this and far more swiftly than you could dream. Your own history tells of many nations that were wrecked, utterly prostrate; yet, within a few years, they recovered and swept over their conquerors."

He indicated Carmody's beltbag and said, "You will hear the last chapter of the Book?"

"On the way back to Earth."

"I do not know why I am not to read it now. But I will find out in good time. Boonta smile upon you, Father. May we meet again under happier conditions. I love you."

He embraced Carmody and wept. Carmody felt his own tears start. He returned his son's kiss and said, "God be with you."

Yess walked out of the port. A bird, a tiny yellow long-beaked creature with black circles around its eyes, swooped by him and uttered seven long notes. Yess made the circular sign at it, but he did not turn around to look again at Carmody. The port swung shut. The priest hurried to his seat to strap himself in, since the takeoff alarm was sounding.

He dropped the spool into the hole by the seat, inserted the earplug, and sat back to listen.

An hour later, the spool was done. With shaking hands, Carmody lit another cigarette.

In exact detail, sometimes naming names and even telling the precise minute, Yess had predicted what would happen. It was all there: the first invasion by the Algulists, their defeat, the second invasion and the unprecedented birth of Algul, Abog's assassination of Rilg, the appearance of the *Argus* (correctly named by Yess and the time of its arrival specified), and the flight in it to the western shore.

Then, using apocalyptic and colorful images, Yess told of the rise of the Boontists from the ashes of the Night and their triumps on other planets of the universe. Everywhere, temples to Boonta would arise, and temples of other gods would crumble.

The final sentence was: "Hear Boonta. The left hand cannot war forever against the right hand."

What did that mean? That Algul would lose to Yess? Or

Yess to Algul? Or—horrifying thought—that the two would join forces and carry all before them?

Carmody replaced the spool in his beltbag. For a moment, he considered destroying it. He shook his head: he would hand the spool over to his superiors. After that, it was up to them to publish it or to keep it secret.

But if they did suppress the Book, they would be admitting that they had reason to fear its contents. If they feared, would it be because, consciously or not, they believed that it might contain the Truth?

He prayed that they would not fear.

After many hours, he fell into an uneasy sleep. A voice awoke him. He started up, thinking for a second that the voice was Mrs. Fratt's. It had faded away during the latter part of the Night. Was it coming back now to torment him? Or was the Goddess speaking to him through Mrs. Fratt, working on his guilt to wear him down?

No. It was his own voice that had been muttering as he came up from the depths.

"What will arise with the waking dreamers? A thing of awesome good, or of awesome evil?"

It was then that a thought that must have been tunneling through the barriers of his mind broke through the wall, and his own black night came upon him.

How could he have seen what he had seen and not believe in the all-power of Boonta? How could he believe that it was only coincidence that he was the first alien Father of the Kareenan god Yess, of Yess who said that Carmody had opened a new path for the worshipers of the Great Mother and that that path was the entire universe? How could he believe that it was only chance that the prophetic Book written by Her son had come into his hands and that he was the instrument to deliver it to the world? Why had he been chosen to witness all this?

That curious happening at Johns Hopkins which had converted him to the faith of the true Church—had it been inspire dand directed by Boonta, so that he might establish himself firmly as a priest in the Church? His belief, which he had thought so strong all these years—had it been sent to him, not by God the Father, but by Boonta the Mother so that he, Carmody, would eventually play Judas?

"Almighty Father!" he prayed aloud. "You know why this has happened! Help me, for I do not know! I have seen things too strong and great for me to resist! You must give me an answer! If ever I needed Your help, it is now!"

160